Ketchup Power
and the
Starship MEATLOAF

OTHER BOOKS YOU WILL ENJOY:

Chocolate Rules and the Starship *Meatloaf,*
Jerry Piasecki

Teacher Vic Is a Vampire . . . Retired,
Jerry Piasecki

Laura for Dessert, *Jerry Piasecki*

The Sixth-Grade Mutants Meet the Slime,
Laura E. Williams

The Chocolate Touch, *Patrick Skene Catling*

Chocolate Fever, *Robert Kimmel Smith*

How to Eat Fried Worms, *Thomas Rockwell*

How to Fight a Girl, *Thomas Rockwell*

Ketchup Power
and the
Starship MEATLOAF

Jerry Piasecki

A Yearling Book

Published by
Bantam Doubleday Dell Books for Young Readers
a division of
Bantam Doubleday Dell Publishing Group, Inc.
1540 Broadway
New York, New York 10036

ISBN: 0-440-41401-6

Printed in the United States of America

October 1997

10 9 8 7 6 5 4 3 2 1

OPM

For Amanda Piasecki and Wendy Rollin

CAST OF CHARACTERS

STARSHIP CREW
Captain Katherine Asher
Dr. Louis J. Kibbleman
Ketchupologist Arlonus Quick
Ketchupologist Theresa Oliver
Android

CURRENT SIXTH GRADERS
Kevin (BB) McKinney
Ellie Fergusan
Perry Hampton
Joyce Chapinski

EVIL LUNCHROOM COOKS
Bertha Butterman
Beula Butterman

COOKING CLASS TEACHER
Mr. Mueller

Ketchup Power
and the
Starship MEATLOAF

One

Day: Wednesday
Time: 10:21 A.M.
Date: The Present

"Wait! Stop! Don't touch that meatloaf!" Louie Droid, one of the new students in Mr. Mueller's sixth-grade cooking class, leaped over a table and snatched a plate of meatloaf from his classmate Ellie Fergusan. As he did, Ellie tried to snatch it back, causing the plate to tip and the meatloaf to slide off.

"No!" Terri and Arlo Droid, two other new students, shouted as they dived for the floor. Arlo came up empty-handed. Terri, however, had a fistful of meatloaf. She jumped triumphantly into the air and shouted, "I got it! I got it!"

"*I* would have had it if you hadn't gotten in my way." Arlo stood up and brushed off his jeans. "You are so competitive."

Terri stuck out her tongue. "Am not!"

"How very adult of you," Arlo huffed. "Don't

you think it's time you acted your age?" He turned and walked away.

"What a sore loser." Terri stuck her tongue out again. She turned to her cooking partner, Kevin McKinney. All the other kids called him BB, short for Big Belly. "You know he's been that way since high school," Terri said to BB.

"High school?" BB scratched the area that had given him his nickname. Whenever BB was confused or scared, he scratched his belly.

"What?" Terri had returned to her mixing bowl.

"You said he's been that way since high school."

"How silly of me," Terri said quickly. "I meant, uh, he's been that way since *pre*-school."

"Oh." BB stopped scratching his belly, remembering that it was a habit he had vowed to break. "That makes more sense . . . I guess."

"Of course it does, silly," Terri said, keeping her eyes focused on her bowl. "After all, we're only in fifth grade."

"We're in *sixth* grade."

"Oh, um . . . that's what I said."

Terri laughed nervously, and BB started to scratch again.

Across the room, Louie was trying to pound some sense into Ellie, who looked at him as if he were a total loon. All she had done was take the meatloaf Mr. Mueller had brought in for show-and-smell out of the refrigerator, and this new kid had gone all-out wacky, trying to grab it from her. Now most of it was on the floor.

"Never, *ever* drop a meatloaf, Ellie," Louie lectured, as he scraped up the mess. "A bruised meatloaf loses seventeen point three percent of its fuel efficiency."

Meanwhile, on the other side of the school, Ms. Millenflower's kindergarten class had gone ballistically bonkers. All at once, every block in the toy box had flown into the air. The blocks floated wildly around the room, coming together to form miniature buildings, spaceships and complete solar systems before bursting apart like Fourth of July fireworks.

The kindergarten students loved the show. They laughed, clapped and squealed happily, grabbing at the blocks as they flew by. Ms. Millenflower, on the other hand, didn't seem to be having as much fun. In fact, she looked whiter than a vampire on a blood-free diet. She kept catching block after block and putting them back into the toy box. But as soon as she put one block away and turned to get another, the first block would float up and rejoin the rest. Ms. Millenflower had no idea what was happening, or why. She did know that the trouble had started immediately after she suggested to the new student, Katherine Droid, that she play with the blocks.

Ms. Millenflower and all the other teachers at Rollindale School knew one other thing. Ever since the Droid kids had enrolled two days earlier, things had taken a distinct turn for the wacky.

Day: Thursday
Time: 1:24 P.M.
Date: October 17, 6789

In the sixty-eighth century, things had quickly gone from wacky to way worse. At first there were just a few minor mishaps. A mechanical dog-walker stopped running, followed almost instantly by its mechanical dog. A boy's Playtime Planet Cruncher stopped in midcrunch. A girl's Barbie Molecular Transporter stopped functioning while she was transporting her newest Skipper doll to a friend's house, causing Moonabu Skipper's molecules to scatter across the Milky Way.

Soon these minor annoyances were replaced by larger problems. The traffic signals between Pluto and Neptune got stuck on green for Pluto, red for Neptune. The next day the European weather dome sprang a leak, and the South American synthesized sun set, never to rise again.

Everything that needed fuel to function—from universe-class starships to lunar jetboards—started to break down. Some things disintegrated on the spot. No one could figure out what in the worlds was going on until one scientist, Dr. Louis J. Kibbleman the 822nd, made a frightful discovery.

It had all started a couple of thousand years earlier, on May 14, 4797, to be exact. On that day, Louis's great-great-great-great-great-great-great-great-great-great-great-great-great-great-etc. grandfather, Dr. Louis J. Kibbleman the 1st, uncovered the most powerful fuel source ever imagined. It was found to be a few zillion times more powerful than coal, oil, nuclear fission or fusion and lead-free Nilarian crystals combined. It was pure power. It was the energy answer. It was a scientist's dream come true. It was . . . ketchup!

The good doctor made his find quite by accident. He had invited a few close friends over for a nice meatloaf dinner. All went well until the next day, when every one of the diners complained bitterly that the main course had given them powerful . . . gas.

After careful investigation, and a mountain of antacids, Louis the 1st determined that it was the ketchup in the meatloaf that actually provided the energy.

What followed was a thousand years of ketchup comfort. The world overflowed with ketchup, and meatloaf factories sprang up on every continent. In its natural state, ketchup is highly unstable as a fuel. It was found to be necessary to house it in meatloaf for maximum safety and fuel efficiency.

Then, in the year 5789, everything changed with the invention of synthochup, a cheap ketchup substitute that seemed to work as well as the real thing. Soon everyone switched to synthochup, and over the centuries the recipe for real ketchup was lost. It was that fact that led to Dr. Louis J. Kibbleman the 822nd's terrible realization. Without real ketchup, the world was in one heck of a pickle.

"It's the synthochup!" Dr. Kibbleman jumped out of his computer and started dancing wildly around the living room with his twelve-year-old daughter, Bianca. Bianca stongly suggested to her father that he get a life.

Dr. Kibbleman ignored the suggestion and called for an emergency meeting of the Earth Select Scientific Council to give his report. "It's the synthochup!" He danced around the podium, causing the council to pass a unanimous resolution that he get a life.

Undaunted, Dr. Kibbleman went on to explain that after years of use, synthochup was actually destroying what it powered. If something wasn't done quickly, the sixty-eighth century would soon be in real danger of grinding to a complete halt.

There was only one possible course of action. Someone would have to attempt to make a perilous backward trip in time and return with the recipe for real, true-red ketchup. The destination would have to be a date when, according to legend, ketchup was available almost anywhere—a time when humans actually used it as a food product instead of as a fuel.

Dr. Kibbleman suggested May 14, 4797. "I'm sure my great-great-great-great-great-great-great-etc. grandfather would be happy to help."

In theory it was possible. In *fact,* nobody knew what would happen if someone tried to travel so far back down Memory Lane. The dangers were many, but the most serious was the Time Porthole Effect experienced in earlier experiments. Time travelers had a specific period during which they could return to their own time. That period was called the porthole. When the porthole closed, the travelers would be trapped in whatever time they had traveled to.

So far, the farthest back anyone had traveled was a day and a half. If they missed the porthole, it wasn't that big a deal. However, going back thousands of years was quite another matter. Nobody knew for sure how long the porthole in time would stay open, but judging from earlier experiments, the most optimistic scientists gave it a week, tops. But, they admitted, only time would tell if they were right.

It was determined that one still-functional starship would attempt to make the journey into the past in order to save the future.

The science starship *Meatloaf* was selected

to do the job. Dr. Kibbleman volunteered to join Captain Asher, two senior ketchupologists and an android called D7 on the mission. The time of departure was set at immediately.

"Time-sequence distributor," Captain Asher said while switching switches and dialing dials.

"Check." Theresa Oliver, one of the ketchupologists, made sure that the right lights were flashing and the wrong ones were not.

"Synthodometer?"

"Check."

The other ketchupologist, Arlonus Quick, was strapped into his seat behind Captain Asher and Theresa Oliver. Dr. Kibbleman's seat was behind his. D7 was a bit overcharged that day and was racing around the starship making last-minute computer adjustments and doing some light dusting.

Everyone was busy trying to be brave, but deep inside they all knew very well that no one had ever done what they were trying to do. They also knew they only had enough synthochup on board for a one-way voyage. They would have to get enough real ketchup, and enough real meatloaf to house it, to get home again with the recipe.

There was also the danger of overshooting their target date and ending up in a land before ketchup. No one was looking forward to spending the rest of their life trying to avoid being a tasty treat for a *Tyrannosaurus rex*.

Finally the checklist had been checked and it was time to go. The crew fell silent. It seemed as if an eternity passed before the order came from the control tower: "Time travelers . . . start your engine."

With a cocky smirk, a confident nod and a slight shiver that she hoped no one saw, Captain Asher lowered her goggles, turned the key in the ignition and pushed down on the accelerator with her right foot. The Starship *Meatloaf* lurched forward. "Let's rock and roll!" she shouted. D7, failing to recognize the meaning of the ancient saying, quickly brought her a kaiser roll and a nice piece of rose quartz.

"Not that kind of rock and roll," she snapped.

"The only other thing I have is a chunk of granite and a little whole wheat," D7 offered.

"Never mind." Captain Asher was trying to concentrate on her driving.

"Sheesh! Make up your mind, why don't you?" D7 pocketed her quartz and kaiser roll and walked away.

Captain Asher pushed down on the accelerator pedal until it almost rested on the floor. Faster and faster the starship flew. First past the speed of sound, then past the speed of light. The captain pushed down harder and the Starship *Meatloaf* entered time warp and the spacetime continuum.

Light like the light of a thousand suns filled the *Meatloaf*. The crew members shut their eyes and covered their faces. When they did, everything went from pure light to total blackness. To each person it seemed as though the ship, and everything else they knew as real, had ceased to exist. Each was alone . . . a prisoner of time.

Captain Asher suddenly saw herself floating in the vast, silent darkness of space. But in this space, all the stars had been replaced by clocks. Clocks of all varieties and descriptions filled her view. From hourglasses to huge tower clocks, from sundials to gold pocket watches, each clock was unique and was set at a different time. Just before everything again faded to black, Captain Asher noticed that despite their many differences, all the clocks had one very unusual thing in common: They were all running backward.

In the utter darkness, Dr. Kibbleman saw his

own face. First it was his face as it had looked when he woke up that morning. Then he watched as his face got younger and younger. In a blink, it was the face of a toddler, then that of a newborn. When the baby opened his eyes, the face became that of a very old man before dissolving into a sparkle of silver dust. The cycle repeated itself over and over again until the face vanished into what Dr. Kibbleman felt was the unmatched comfort of the deepest night.

Theresa Oliver spun through time like a flaming comet. She darted past an endless array of stars and planets of every hue. Ahead, or was it behind, she saw a beautiful blue world. It got closer and closer until she was almost there. Then nothing but the ever-present blackness closed in from all sides.

Arlonus Quick giggled and then laughed out loud. The darkness wrapped around his body. It tickled everywhere it touched. He saw his mother and father laughing. For a moment he saw his great-aunt, his great-great-uncle, and his great-great-great-grandmother in near hysterics. He saw people he didn't recognize but whom he felt he knew. Each one laughed along with him. Then, as fast as it had begun, the laughter stopped and only the darkness remained.

To each crew member it seemed as though

only a split split second had passed before they lowered their hands from their faces and opened their eyes again. They were still securely in their seats, safely on board the *Meatloaf*. But, oddly, the cabin now appeared somewhat bigger and the control panels larger than they had been before. Dr. Kibbleman was the first to look up at his companions. In a shaky voice, which he barely recognized as having once been his own, he stated what would soon be obvious to all.

"Ah, people . . . I think we have a problem."

Two

"Oh, my . . . Ouch!" Arlonus leaped out of his chair and tripped over his pants legs, which were now at least a foot too long. He bopped his nose against a control panel before tumbling to the floor of the *Meatloaf*. His legs, arms and body were trapped in a tangled heap of fabric, zippers, buttons and badges.

Theresa turned and laughed loudly at the sight of her fellow ketchupologist rolling on the floor in mortal combat with his own uniform. Then she happened to get a sideways glance at her own reflection in one of the *Meatloaf*'s observation windows. Theresa stopped laughing. She turned for a better look. She started to scream.

Dr. Kibbleman had rolled up his pants legs and shirtsleeves. He had also tightened his belt eight notches so that his pants had a fighting chance to stay on. He knew he had to stop Theresa's screaming and Arlonus's battle with his britches. How to do it was another story. One thought kept running through the doctor's mind. He started singing a rousing chorus of "Kumbaya" at the top of his lungs.

It worked. Theresa's mouth snapped shut, and Arlonus stopped his struggling and peeked out from his shirt collar. They looked at Dr. Kibbleman as if he had gone three-quarters crazy and one-quarter nuts.

"Sorry." Dr. Kibbleman stopped singing after finishing the verse. "I couldn't think of anything else to do."

"Next time," Theresa said as she put her hands on Dr. Kibbleman's shoulders, "try harder."

"What's happened to us?" Arlonus had stumbled to his feet, tripped over his now too-long pants and struggled up once more. "I think I shrank."

"I was afraid of this." Dr. Kibbleman examined Theresa's teeth and plucked a hair from Arlonus's head.

"Ouch!" Arlonus yelled. He pointed at Theresa. "Take *her* hair."

"Not my hair." Theresa ran her fingers through her hair, which was much longer than it had been when she had brushed it an hour ago. It was now the exact length it had been when she was . . .

"Twelve years old!" Dr. Kibbleman exclaimed. He held the hair up to the light to reconfirm his findings. "When we went back in time, we got younger. We're all twelve years old again."

"Not all of us." A high-pitched voice came from the other side of the captain's seat, which slowly swiveled around. "Some of us are a bit younger."

When Captain Asher came into view, it was a captain that none of the crew had seen before. The legs of her uniform draped off the chair and dangled to the floor. The arms hung limply at the sides of the chair, swaying slightly. The captain looked like a rag doll in a real person's clothing.

Captain Asher was known as one of the strictest, most no-nonsense officers in the Science Fleet. Her new freckles, dimples and missing front tooth tended to undermine her authority.

"I want some explanations," Captain Asher snapped, jumping down from her seat. As she spoke, she gave a slight whistle from the gap where her front tooth was missing. "And I want those explanations now."

The rest of the crew members tried to stifle their laughter at the sight of a pigtailed, five-year-old captain marching around the *Meatloaf* in an oversized uniform, demanding answers and giving orders.

When no one said a word, the captain climbed onto a chair, stood as tall as she could, folded her little arms and said, "Well, I'm waiting."

Dr. Kibbleman, Theresa and Arlonus lost it. They fell to the floor laughing. Fortunately for them, D7 stepped forward and saved the day.

"I saw the whole thing." The android, who had not been affected by the time travel, spoke quickly. "And I don't mind telling you that if I hadn't seen it with my own fiber-optic visual-reception units, I wouldn't have believed it."

"What did you see?" Captain Asher prompted. She knew that D7 had a minor computer glitch that often prevented her from getting right to the point. It was something the captain had always intended to have fixed—as soon as there was time.

"Do you want the long or short version?" D7 asked.

"Short."

"Okay." D7 was disappointed but not surprised. "Arlonus was right . . . you shrank." The android looked at the captain. "You just shrank a little more than the rest."

"Look at that!" Theresa had walked over to one of the *Meatloaf*'s observation windows.

Everyone followed and looked. They saw a beautiful blue planet far below. Arlonus recognized the coast of Africa as they passed above, and then the approaching coast of North America. "Well," he said. "At least we know *where* we are."

"True." Captain Asher nodded as she strained her neck to see over the windowsill. "But there's still one very big question."

"And that is?" Theresa asked.

"What time is it?"

"Judging from the lack of space traffic," Dr. Kibbleman said softly, "I'd say it's a long, long time ago."

"The dayometer says it's Sunday," Arlonus called from the other end of the *Meatloaf*. He carefully checked, and rechecked, the equipment.

"What *year*?" Captain Asher asked, striding over to Arlonus.

"I think you'd better look for yourself."

When the three human crew members and one android looked over Arlonus's shoulder, they all said the exact same thing: "Oh, wow."

"And how, 'oh, wow.'" Arlonus checked to make sure the equipment was functioning properly. "Looks as if we missed our target by only a couple of thousand years."

"So much for asking my great-great-great-great-great-great-etc. grandfather for help," Dr. Kibbleman said. "What should we do now?"

"The first thing we should do is land the *Meatloaf*," said Captain Asher. She walked back to her chair and climbed on. She had to sit on the very edge and stretch forward to reach the controls.

"Where do we land?" Theresa asked.

"Well," Captain Asher said, glancing at her traveling companions and then at herself, "in our present states, I suggest we look for a place with a good school system."

Day: Sunday
Time: 8:26 P.M.
Date: The Present

Ellie Fergusan and Kevin "BB" McKinney hated Sunday nights. They signaled the end of the weekend, with nothing to look forward to but getting up early for school the next morning. This particular Sunday night was worse than most because their math teacher, Mr. Neuhauser, had scheduled a test for first thing Monday.

Ellie and BB had just finished studying with their friends, Perry Hampton and Joyce Chapinski, who secretly liked each other but refused to admit it. Ellie and BB had been neighbors since birth, and friends since shortly thereafter.

"I think Monday-morning tests should be against the law," Ellie complained as they cut through the school playground on the way to their houses.

"Yeah." BB nodded. "I don't start thinking until Tuesday afternoon at the earliest."

"The *very* earliest," Ellie agreed.

"Maybe not until Wednesday . . . after lunch."

"I have a great number for that math teacher," Ellie said. "How about *twenty* years in jail for being mean to students?"

"*Twenty-five* is a better number," BB offered.

"Or *thirty*."

Ellie and BB kept adding on numbers. They

didn't stop until they reached 980. "That should be long enough," BB said.

"Yeah." Ellie smiled at the thought. "We don't want to go overboard. After all, it's only a test."

BB was about to point out that this was Mr. Neuhauser's second or third offense, when both he and Ellie froze in their tracks. A flash of brilliant light streaked directly overhead and disappeared behind a cluster of trees at the other end of the playground.

"Did you see that?" BB yelled.

"Did you?" Ellie's voice quaked.

"What, uh, should we do?" BB scratched his belly harder than he'd ever scratched before.

"I have an idea," Ellie said.

"Wh-What?"

"Run!"

Three

Day: Monday
Time: 9:07 A.M.
Date: The Present

"I want to enroll my twin sets of twins for school," a very mechanical, semifemale voice said. The woman who faced Principal Walters in his small office at Rollindale Elementary School acted bright and cheerful, but her skin was gray, her handshake was like a steel vise and she was wearing a blazing red wig.

What Principal Walters found most strange were the woman's eyes. Every few seconds they seemed to light up with a different color. First they were blue, then red, then yellow. The process repeated itself for several minutes until the woman noticed Principal Walters staring. D7 quickly put on a pair of dark sunglasses. "My eyes are still adjusting to the drops the eye doctor put in them this morning," she said crisply.

"Ahhh." Principal Walters smiled. "That explains it."

Principal Walters always searched for a logical explanation. When he found one, he clung to it like a pit bull on a pork chop, no matter how illogical it was to do so.

"So, Ms. um . . . Ms. um . . . Ms. . . ." Principal Walters had forgotten the woman's name.

"Droid," she said. "Ann Droid."

"Of course, Ms. Droid." Principal Walters smiled a sickly sweet smile that no student ever saw. It was reserved for parents only. "You say you have twin sets of twins that you'd like to enroll?"

D7 nodded, which caused a loud squeaking sound. "I must see my chiropractor," she said quickly, thinking that she was long overdue for a good oiling.

"Twin sets of twins . . . I can't say I've ever heard of such a thing."

"They are somewhat unusual," D7 agreed.

"I'd love to meet them."

"Of course."

As if they had heard the entire conversation, which they had because D7 had kept her communicator on, the "twin sets of twins" immediately walked into the office. Principal Walters stared at the three twelve-year-olds and the one five-year-old. "I thought you said they were twins."

"I never said they were *identical.*" D7 couldn't believe how dense some humans were.

Principal Walters decided against pursuing the point. He never asked a question when he really didn't want to know the answer. "Well, anyway, let me greet our four new students." Principal Walters walked around his desk and shook hands with the tallest boy. "What's your name, son?"

"Dr. Louis J. Kibbleman the eight hundred twenty-second."

"Huh?"

Oops, Dr. Kibbleman thought. "Louie," he said clearly. "I meant to say that my name is Louie, Louie Droid."

"And I'm Terri Droid," said Theresa, smiling.

"Arlo Droid. Pleased to meet you," said Arlonus.

"Captain Droid. At your service, sir," lisped Captain Asher.

Principal Walters looked down at the saluting five-year-old. "Excuse me?"

"She meant *Katherine,*" Louie covered for his captain.

"I love the name Katherine," Principal Walters said. "May I call you Katie, cutie?"

"Absolutely not!"

A fake last name like *Droid* was one thing, but a sweet nickname was more than the kindergarten captain could bear. As for calling her *cutie,* it was very lucky for the principal that the captain had left her phaser on board the *Meatloaf.*

"Ha. Ha." Ann Droid pronounced every *ha* carefully. "Little Katherine is such a . . ." She searched her dictionary of ancient human terms, ". . . carp."

"You're calling your child a carp?" Principal Walters looked concerned.

Whoops, too far in the dictionary. Ann Droid ran the internal document backward. "She's such a *card.* Ha. Ha. Ha. Not carp . . . *card.*"

This was one odd family, Principal Walters thought. He had seen unusual students before. There was the Belker boy, six years ago, who tried to convince his teacher that he turned into a largemouth bass on weekends, so he couldn't do his homework. Then, of course, there were the Clauson kids, who claimed to be every religion on earth so that they could celebrate all the holidays by staying home. Principal Walters knew that the Droids would join his own private list of America's Most Weird.

In addition to everything else, the kids' clothing looked like sewn-up, taken-in, shortened and stapled-shut space suits. The mother was wearing a dress made out of a blanket, with an extension cord tied around the middle for a belt. Principal Walters also thought the mother seemed a bit stiff and mechanical, but he figured that might have been from the eyedrops. Anyway, that's what he chose to believe.

"Welcome to Rollindale School." He ushered the new students toward his office door. "The school secretary will show you to your classes. Katherine, you'll be in Ms. Millenflower's kindergarten. Terri, Arlo and Louie, I think we'll keep you three together in Ms. Neff's homeroom."

"What's a homeroom?" Arlo asked.

"Shhh, stupid," Terri whispered. "It's obviously a room where you learn about homes."

"Oh, one more thing . . ." Principal Walters paused. "As sixth-graders, the three of you get to choose between taking shop and . . . cooking."

The decision to take cooking was quick and unanimous. The *Meatloaf* crew's plan was working out much better than expected. To fit in and not arouse suspicion, they had decided to attend school during the day and find somewhere to make meatloaf at night, since ovens were not standard equipment on a starship. Now it appeared that the time travelers would be able to cook at school, and get their beauty sleep after all.

Day: Wednesday
Time: 10:25 A.M.
Date: The Present

"You see, Ellie," Louie said as he followed Ellie back to the table where she sat with Joyce, "if not properly handled, the meatloaf itself can be almost as unpredictable as the ketchup."

Ellie hid behind Joyce. "Uh, Louie?"

"Yes?"

"What are you talking about?"

Louie was about to explain the Theory of Ketchuptivity, $E=MK^2$, when he remembered that he would be over four thousand years ahead of himself. From the looks on Joyce's and Ellie's faces, he might also end up being locked in a padded cell until the day he would be born.

"I have no idea," he said.

"That makes two of us," Ellie said.

"Make that three of us," Joyce joined in.

Before Louie could talk himself into deeper trouble, he learned the lesson in the ancient Earth saying "Saved by the bell."

The ringing of the bell after cooking class was always followed by another sound. *"Lunch!"* BB yelled each and every day—same time, same place.

BB always said that lunch was his favorite school subject. He was very good at it. If reading, writing and arithmetic were ever replaced by eating, biting and arithma-lick, he'd be an A+ student.

As usual, Mr. Mueller had to sprint like a world-class Olympian to beat BB to the door and block his path to pleasure. He spoke quickly, knowing full well that standing between BB and his baloney was, at best, a risky business.

"Remember, everyone," Mr. Mueller called out. "You all must bring in a meatloaf recipe for class tomorrow."

All but three members of the class groaned. Those three were yelling and cheering. It had been their idea to study meatloaf, and Mr. Mueller had instantly and enthusiastically gone along with the new kids' idea.

"Stop!" Ms. Millenflower sat on the kinder-garten floor while laughing students and floating blocks danced around her. "Stop-stop-stop-stop-stop-stop-*stop!*"

Across the room, Katherine Droid figured that the teacher had learned her lesson. She reached into her pocket and pushed the middle button on her portable transpondilator. Instantly all the blocks fell to the floor, which caused the kindergartners to stop laughing. Ms. Millen-flower looked at Katherine, who just shrugged. *That'll teach you to tell a starship captain to play with blocks,* Katherine thought.

Before Ms. Millenflower could ask her new student what she was holding in her pocket, the bell rang. It signaled the end of the kindergart-ner's day, the start of a quick trip to the psychia-trist for the teacher, and lunch for everyone else.

Mr. Mueller smiled after all the students, with BB in the lead, had filed out the door. He had always prided himself on his meatloaf and was delighted to have an opportunity to show it off. He had the new students to thank. They had suggested that meatloaf was the perfect food for learning to cook.

"You have to mix all sorts of things," Louie had said.

"And crack eggs," Terri added.

"And put in spices," Arlo said.

"And pour *ketchup!*" all three students shouted.

Mr. Mueller clapped his hands and cheered.

Once all his students had left for lunch, Mr. Mueller whistled as he wondered what kind of meatloaf recipes the class would bring in, particularly the new students. They showed real promise. Mr. Mueller thought they might be the kind of students he'd been waiting for, for a long, long time.

He happily searched for the plate to which Terri and Louie had returned the meatloaf so that he could put it in the fridge and get his lunch. When he found it, he stopped smiling. The plate was there, but the meatloaf was gone. *Oh well,* he thought, *BB must have been the bandit. I guess I can't blame the boy. After all, we are talking about my delicious meatloaf.*

Happy again, Mr. Mueller got his sandwich

out of his lunch bag and took a big hearty bite of—bread.

"What the—?" Mr. Mueller peeked between the slices and almost started to cry. His meatloaf sandwich was mysteriously missing one very important ingredient—meatloaf.

Four

Louie, Arlo and Terri were the last to leave Mr. Mueller's classroom for lunch. As they walked down the hall, Louie whispered to Terri, "Did you get it?"

She patted her Neptunian quartz lunch box. "Yup."

"How about you?" Louie turned to Arlo, who felt warm mayonnaise soaking through his pants pocket and oozing down his left leg.

"Yeah, I got it all right. I really got it." Arlo shook his left leg as he walked. He felt a glop of gooey mayonnaise drop down into his sock. "But I'll tell you one thing: That teacher is a barbarian. I mean, whoever heard of putting mayo on meatloaf? It'll jam up the engines for sure."

"Remember, Arlonus," Louie whispered. "These people still consider meatloaf nothing

32

more than food. They really are quite primitive."

Louie didn't know it at the time, but he and his companions were about to discover exactly how "primitive" certain people could be.

"Get that shrimp out of here," Beula Butterman sneered. She swiped at the sweat dripping from her upper lip.

"Yeah." Her sister Bertha, the other lunchroom cook, belched. She pointed at Katherine, who had joined her crew in the cafeteria line. "We ain't serving shrimps today. They ain't on the menu."

While the Buttermans laughed, Katherine decided to try the polite route. "May I *please* have some lunch?" she said sweetly.

"Hey, Beula," Bertha said, and laughed even louder, "the shrimp said *pllll-eeeeeeease.*"

"Oh, well, seeing as how she said *pllll-eeeeeeease,* our answer will have to be—"

Beula and Bertha stopped laughing. They looked at each other, then back at Katherine, before snapping out a joint *"No!"*

Bertha and Beula Butterman were the most beastly of bullies. They'd been that way since they were old enough to yank a cat's tail. All that had happened in the years that followed was that they had gone from being tiny bullies to being tall ones.

Each sister had broken teeth, strong buffalo breath and some most unpleasant digestive problems. They washed their hair twice a year, whether it needed it or not. They washed their feet even less often. Bertha had a huge mole with two long red hairs sticking out in the middle of her forehead. Beula's mole, which rested on the right side of her chin, had six hairs, three white and three black, which she occasionally braided and tied with tiny pink ribbons. They were the envy of every Butterman anywhere in the world.

Bertha weighed in at 396 pounds. Beula had recently broken her doctor's scale. Both had the personalities of piranhas and the tempers of two-year-olds in all-out tantrum. They were not very nice people.

Ever since she was first able to ride a starcycle, Katherine had had a serious problem with people who were "not nice." She reached into her pocket and placed her finger on her transpondilator's second button.

"Beat it, shrimp-boat!" Beula spit. "No kindergartners allowed."

Katherine moved her finger to the first button. Before she had a chance to turn the cooks into croutons, Ellie stepped between them.

"Please excuse them, Ms. Buttermans," Ellie said. She thought the new kids were weird, but nobody deserved to be the target of the Butterman twins. "They're new. They don't know your rules."

"That's no skin off our hot dogs," Beula barked.

"Yeah, they should know our food is rated R." Bertha's nostrils flared. "No one under six allowed."

"The *R* is for *rancid*," BB whispered to Louie. He had reluctantly put his baloney on hold to join the group.

"Or for *rotten*," Perry whispered into Louie's other ear.

"Or for the *runs*," Joyce whispered a bit too loudly.

"What was that?" Bertha and Beula snarled together.

"Uhhhh, uhhhhh . . ." Joyce stammered and stuttered until Ellie made her second save of the lunch hour.

"She said, Feed the runt this time so that she'll know what she's missing every day for the rest of the school year," Ellie said.

"Is that what you said?" Bertha demanded.

"Uh . . . yes?" Joyce's voice quivered.

Beula and Bertha looked at Joyce. They were impressed.

"Good girl." Bertha patted Joyce on the head, making her hair smell like month-old greaseburgers.

"We like the way you think." When Beula spoke, bits of her breakfast shot out of her mouth and around the room. "Maybe we'll make you our lunchroom helper."

Joyce dropped her tray and ran away.

"I guess all the excitement was too much for her." Beula laughed.

"Here, runt." Bertha slopped a huge portion of the house specialty onto a plate and shoved it at Katherine. "Enjoy."

"What is it?" Katherine asked.

"It's our world-famous spaghetti and beet-balls, of course." Bertha sounded hurt. She and her sister started to walk back toward the other side of the kitchen. "You ungrateful little runt-rodent."

"Did you call me a runt-rodent?" Katherine called after the Buttermans.

"Of course not," Bertha said. "I called you a shrimp-brained, jerk-nosed, dirty-diapered runt-rodent."

As Beula gave Bertha a high five, Katherine

pushed the second button. Instantly hundreds of beetballs blasted out of the huge pot in which they'd been boiled. They flew through the air and bashed against Bertha and Beula, covering them from their hair buns to their blistering bunions. Both sisters were knocked to the floor, where they sat bottom deep in beets.

"See, I told you." Bertha mushed a handful of beets into Beula's hair. "Too much paprika."

One final beetball shot across the kitchen and spattered full force on Bertha's nose. Her tongue darted out and caught a few drops of sauce. "*Way* too much paprika," she agreed.

Everyone in the lunchroom gave the show a standing ovation. The applause didn't stop until the Buttermans scrambled to their feet. They threatened to make every student eat beetaroni and cheese for the next month. That was enough to make everyone stop clapping and become slightly nauseated.

As Bertha and Beula scraped the beets from the floor for Friday's cook's choice lunch, Ellie invited Katherine, Louie, Arlo and Terri to join her and her friends at their table. "Did you have anything to do with that?" she said, looking from Katherine to the kitchen and back again.

"No!" Katherine and her entire crew shouted at the same time.

"Easy."

Ellie held up her hands. "Just asking. Like, cool your jets, okay?"

"Why? Are they overheating?" Katherine checked her sneakers to make sure she hadn't accidentally left them on after landing near school that morning.

"Where did you guys say you were from?" Ellie asked.

"A place a lot like this one," Louie said.

"Is it far?" Joyce asked.

"Let's just say it would take quite a while to get there."

BB looked at the foursome warily. As far as he was concerned, there were still some very important questions to ask before he would welcome these new kids as friends. "Take your pick, white bread or wheat?"

When he didn't get an immediate reply, BB went on to question number two.

"Are you cake people or pie people?" BB thought you could tell a lot about a person by whether they'd describe themselves as preferring cakes or pies.

"Would you please shut up?" Ellie asked.

"I'd expect that from a pie person," BB said, glaring at Ellie. He was about to ask his question again, but the lunch bell rang. Without hesitating, BB stuffed half a sandwich, two Fruit Roll-Ups, thirty-seven Doritos, a bag of Skittles and eight Snackwell's fat-free cookies into his mouth. For BB it wasn't much of a challenge.

"You guys want to hang out later?" Ellie asked. She had decided that these new kids were probably okay.

"Sure," Louie said. He had absolutely no idea what Ellie was talking about, but thought it would be a good idea to accept the invitation in order to learn more about these ancient students.

"Cool," Ellie said. "Come over to my house at about six-thirty. My mom will drive us to the mall."

"Cool," Arlo said, extremely proud of his grasp of this long-forgotten human language. "In fact, I'd say it's downright cold."

"Uhhhh, yeah. Rrrr-ight." Ellie smiled and backed away. "See you later."

"Frozen!" Arlo smiled.

On their way to class all four time travelers had the same troubling thought: *What the heck is a mall?*

Five

After school the crew rushed home to the Starship *Meatloaf,* which D7 had disguised to look like a regular ranch house. She was a whiz at hologram camouflage. No one seeing the starship from the outside would think it was anything but an ordinary, peaceful home. Inside, however, things were far from normal.

"And who's going to drive?"

"Ellie's mom." Louie answered D7's question.

"What time will you be home?"

"By nine o'clock at the latest," Terri promised.

"What about your homework?"

"Stop!" Captain Asher spun around in her captain's chair. She looked tiny in the huge seat, with her feet dangling off the edge. "That's quite enough, D7."

"Call me Mama."

"D7," the captain repeated. "We have to blend into this century. Everyone, except you, is going to the mall."

"And I suppose if everyone was going to jump off the cliffs on a Rogarian moon, you would too?"

"*D7.*" Captain Asher's voice sounded threatening. She stood up on her chair. "Remember whom you're talking to."

"I suggest you do the same, young lady."

"I'm the captain on this mission." Captain Asher stamped her foot.

"I'm the mother," Ann Droid proclaimed. "And mothers outrank captains any day."

D7 was taking her role as the mother of twin sets of twins to mechanical heart. "Anyway," she said, "what about your dinner?"

"You didn't cook anything," Arlo said.

"You always have an answer for everything, don't you, young man?"

"Let's go," Captain Asher said. "Remember to bring your phasers. We don't know if this mall thing is dangerous."

The last words they heard from D7 as they

walked out of the *Meatloaf* were, "Kids, they just don't listen nowadays."

"Set to stun! *Open fire!*"

At the mall, things had gotten way out of control. Ellie's, BB's, Joyce's and Perry's mouths dropped open as the new kids pulled what looked like little crystal water pistols out of their pockets. In stunned silence they watched Katherine roll under a bench and Louie jump behind a big potted palm tree.

"Get down, you guys!" Arlo yelled as he and Terri knocked the shocked sixth-graders to the floor. They landed between a trash can and a pile of trash. Arlo jumped on top of BB and Joyce, and Terri did the same to Ellie and Perry. Both tried to cover their new friends to protect them from what they viewed as an extremely dangerous situation.

"Stay down," Terri said. "This looks really bad."

Katherine and her crew pointed their crystal pistols at the Sears display windows and pulled the triggers. Rays of light, each a different color, shot from the guns. The green, orange, red and purple rays streaked toward the windows just as

one of the decorators removed the upper torso
and head of a mannequin.

"Too late!" Katherine cried. "He got another
one."

All the way to the mall, the four time travelers
had felt like screaming. They'd been somewhat
nervous about piling into the small thin metal-
and-plastic vehicle with the four circular rubber
things on each corner. Ellie's mom had called it
"the van." It appeared to be far less structurally
sound than even a used starship on a discount
space lot.

Their emotions raced quickly past fear and
terror before settling close to all-out panic when
they saw that "the van" had to share a narrow
concrete path with thousands and thousands of
similar vehicles. Each one was traveling at a different speed in a different direction. Each one
also appeared to be piloted by a complete idiot.
In fact, that was the phrase screamed out the
window by Ellie's mom when one such driver
pulled directly into their path.

When they finally made it to a huge structure,
which they were able to identify by the sign
reading TWIN PINES MALL, the four tumbled out of

the van as quickly as possible. While Katherine, Louie and Terri tried to slow their heart rates down to light speed, Arlo fell to his hands and knees and kissed the ground, grateful to be alive.

All four were all smiles until they heard Ellie's mom say, "I'll pick you up right here at eight-fifteen. Don't be late."

"You mean we have to go back home in that thing?" Katherine pointed at the van.

"How else are we going to get home?" BB asked. "Fly?"

Katherine looked down at her jet sneakers. "Sounds good to me."

All the present-day sixth-graders laughed at what they thought was the kindergartner's little joke. None of the time travelers even cracked a smile. They knew that Katherine had been totally serious.

After a short period of adjustment, the future foursome started to enjoy the mall. They had never seen anything like it, with its rows and rows of strange shops featuring historical clothing, primitive devices and ancient artifacts. To them it was like being in a gigantic museum where everything was for sale.

"This place is an archaeologist's dream come true," Louie whispered to Arlo. He didn't know it, but around the next corner, all his dreams would become a brutal, barbaric nightmare.

When they saw what was happening, they couldn't believe their eyes. There they were, right in the store window—people viciously tearing apart other people as if for the sheer pleasure of it. Even more frightening was the fact that no one in the mall seemed to be paying any attention.

One of the people in the window removed the arms of a woman. Another snapped off a man's legs. The victims had apparently been frozen stiff by some sort of paralyzing weapon and were unable to resist. Captain Asher knew that action had to be taken before anyone else got hurt. That was when she gave the order to open fire.

The first ray shot through the window, vaporizing the glass. The closest decorator was hit right in the belly button by the next ray. He dropped the torso he was holding before falling to the floor, dazed and confused. Another decorator tried to run, but he was hit with a red ray in the backside. The third decorator darted behind a pile of plastic arms and legs.

"Move in," Katherine ordered. "There's still one left."

With most of the decorators down, Arlo and Terri got up and slowly approached the window, phasers armed and ready to fire.

Ellie and BB scrambled to their feet. "What are you guys doing?" Ellie stood with hands on hips, shocked at the scene that was unfolding before her.

"Get down," Katherine ordered. "There's one more."

"One more what?" Ellie demanded. She was confused, concerned and really embarrassed.

"One more of those terror troopers. Didn't you see what they were doing to those people?"

Ellie looked toward the window. "Those are mannequins."

"Who cares what planet they're from? They're still people," the captain said.

"No, they're not." Ellie shook her head.

"Then what are they?"

"They're plastic."

"They're . . . plastic?" Katherine slowly lowered her phaser.

Ellie looked at BB, who looked at Joyce, who

looked at Perry. None of them said a word. They didn't have to.

"I guess you think we have a little explaining to do, huh?" Louie asked.

"I'd say more like a lot of explaining," Ellie said.

"A lot of a lot," BB added.

"Uhh, I think that's going to have to wait," Joyce said nervously.

"Why?" BB asked.

"Look!" Perry answered.

They all saw mall Security racing toward them from three different directions. It was obvious that the best course of action would be to run in the only direction left open to them—straight toward the Sears window.

The two stunned decorators were starting to regain their senses, while the third was losing his composure. As Louie, Ellie, and the rest of the kids ran through the window, the decorator shrieked loudly and raced off into the mall. He slammed directly into the first two security officers, sending them flying into the two behind them. By the time the guards got up, the four students and the four time travelers had raced through Sears and were halfway to BB's favorite hiding place . . . McDonald's.

As the group approached the restaurant, everyone except BB stopped running. BB ran faster. Louie, Katherine, Arlo and Terri had seen some strange things in this ancient time, but nothing had prepared them for what they were about to discover.

Inside the restaurant, the kids caught their breaths and approached the counter. None of the time travelers had any idea what the words on the wall menu meant, so Katherine, being the first of them to order, just asked for the same as BB. He had beaten the others to the restaurant in order to secure the first place in line.

The person behind the counter looked a bit surprised that a kindergartner would order two Quarter Pounders, two large fries, two apple pies and two chocolate shakes.

"Are you sure you're going to be able to eat all that, cutie?" the counterperson asked.

Katherine wasn't in the mood to be accused of being cute for the second time in one mission. "Didn't you understand my order?" she snapped.

"Uh, yeah. I understood it." The counterperson was startled by the authority in the girl's voice.

"Then follow it." Because of his uniform,

Katherine assumed the counterperson was in some branch of the military. "Or I'll have you court-martialed."

"Okay, okay," the counterperson said as he started to fill Katherine's order. "Do you need salt or ketchup?"

"Ketchup!" Katherine answered quickly and loudly.

The counterperson put two tiny packets of ketchup on Katherine's tray. When she didn't move away he asked, "Do you want some more?"

"Yes," Katherine answered. "A lot more."

Katherine didn't leave the counter until the worker had loaded her tray with thirty-seven packets of ketchup. She would have asked for more, but she didn't want to attract attention.

Then it was Arlo's turn to order. "I'll have what she had." He jerked a thumb in Katherine's direction. "Only this time, start with the ketchup."

By the time Terri and Louie had ordered and joined the rest, the four had collected 159 packets of ketchup.

"This will make enough meatloaf to get to the Andromeda Nebula," Katherine said. She was so excited that she actually giggled.

"I love these travel packets." Louie examined one of the ketchups. "Ingenious!"

"It's just ketchup," Perry said.

"A whole mountain of ketchup," Joyce corrected.

"Do you want to tell us what's going on?" Ellie took a sip of her Coke. "And about those ray-gun thingies you almost blew up the mall with?"

BB seconded Ellie's question with a nod and a noise. He already had half a Quarter Pounder and a slurp of shake in his mouth. BB hated to talk with his mouth full. He considered it a horrendous waste of valuable eating time.

For the next half hour Louie and his traveling companions told their new friends a story that made even BB forget about his burger.

Six

The time travelers had spilled the beans. They'd talked about everything from that first taste of ketchup power to the discovery of the destructive properties of synthochup. They'd talked about the need for meatloaf as a means of housing the volatile fuel source, and about how the fate of the future rested on their shoulders. They had also said they could use some help.

The reaction from the present-day sixth-graders had ranged from Joyce's confused "Say what?" to Perry's sarcastic "Yeah, like rrr-riiiight."

"We can prove it to you," Katherine had said. "You can come to our starship and see for yourself."

"But you have to promise not to tell anyone," Louie had warned.

"You mean about ketchup being the fuel of the future?" Perry had rolled his eyes. "Don't worry." He'd laughed. "I won't."

"It couldn't hurt to see their place," BB said. He sort of believed the story.

"Yeah, he's right," Ellie said. She didn't know what to believe, but she couldn't get the ray-gun scene out of her mind.

"Okay, I'll go," Perry said. "But I think it's all a big bunch of baloney."

"Sounds good to me." BB felt his stomach rumble at the mention of one of his favorite foods.

By the time BB, Perry and Joyce called home to say they'd be a little late, it was eight-fifteen and time to meet Ellie's mother. It took a fair amount of convincing to get her to drop the group off at the Droids' house.

"Our androi—mom—will bring them home by nine. Promise," Louie said.

"Are you sure she's home and won't mind all of you invading your house?"

"For positive sure. It'll be chilly with her," Arlo said.

Ellie's mom felt much better about the whole thing when she pulled up in front of the Droids' home. It was in a wooded area, in a neighborhood close to the school. The house looked immaculate and in great repair. Not a single brick or blade of grass was broken, bent or even slightly out of place.

"Your parents keep this place in terrific shape," Ellie's mom said. She was impressed— and a little jealous, remembering the disaster zone that awaited her at home. "It must keep them busy."

"Oh." Katherine smiled. "Mom's a real machine."

"She must be." Ellie's mom shook her head.

"Trust me." Katherine's smile broadened. "She is."

As everyone got out of the car, Ellie's mother made her daughter promise to call if they couldn't get a ride. As it turned out, that was not going to be a problem.

"This is your starship?" BB sounded really disappointed.

"See?" Perry said in an I-told-you-so voice. "These kids are pranking us big-time. There's no starship."

The group stood in front of a yellow-brick, one-story ranch house. The house was about as regular as you can get, right down to its welcome mat.

"What a rip-off." Perry feigned anger, but secretly he felt proud that he was the only one who knew it had been a scam all along. "*Total* rip-off." Perry repeated his point while stepping up onto the house's porch. "Whoever heard of a brick starship?"

For dramatic effect Perry hit his hand against the house. When he did, he let out a little scared squeak and yanked his hand away. He had expected to feel the rough texture of bricks. Instead, he felt the smooth, cold hardness of pure metal.

"Right this way, please," Katherine said while opening the screen door. "Welcome to the *Meatloaf*. Watch your step."

When she opened the screen door there was a loud hissing sound and a puff of smoke. Suddenly several silver steps descended. The four students moved back quickly and would have fallen off the porch if a gentle force field hadn't stopped them.

"After you." Katherine gestured toward the steps.

One by one the group climbed the stairs from the porch to the starship. This time the four present-day sixth-graders had the same reaction: "Oh, wow!"

In a few short steps they had gone forward almost five thousand years. Instead of the living-room-on-the-right, kitchen-straight-ahead floor plan they'd expected, the students saw curved metal walls with panel after panel of controls, flashing lights and computer screens. They saw a sign reading DANGER—ANTIMATTER CONTAINMENT FIELD near the rear door, and a 3-D map of the universe floating in what looked like a huge fortune-teller's crystal ball.

"B-B-B-B-B-But, what about the house?" Perry turned around slowly to take in the entire starship. Then he turned around again, and again.

"That's just a hologram," Terri said. "We didn't think a starship would fit in with the neighborhood."

"I voted for a high-rise apartment building," Arlo complained. "But no. They had to have a house hologram. I mean, a fifty-thousand-story apartment building hologram would have been totally brisk."

"Brisk?" Ellie asked while examining the synthochup guage, which rested on E.

Before Arlo could explain that he was just cool-talking, the conversation was interrupted by a frantic call.

"Help!" screamed BB in absolute terror. "It's eating me!"

BB had wandered away from the group to try out the captain's chair. When he first sat down it felt hard and bumpy. He started to reach for the armrests to give himself a boost, when the armrests reached for him. They shot out and grabbed him in a big chair *hug.*

BB felt the back, seat and sides of the chair envelop him completely. He started to scream when he felt a kind of chewing motion inside the chair. For the first time BB thought he knew what it felt like to be lunch.

Before BB had time to scream again, the chair bloomed, opening like the petals of a flower. All at once BB realized that he had never been so comfortable in his entire life.

"Sorry." Katherine walked over. "I should have warned you that we have biocomfort seats. They conform to the shape, temperature and mood of the person sitting in them."

"I'll say." BB smiled. "Can I borrow one for school?"

"I think someone might notice," Perry said.

"Yeah, but who cares?"

BB felt the chair changing shape ever so slightly, adjusting to his every movement. Each position was as comfortable as the one before, which was the most comfortable ever.

Just then the door hissed open and D7 walked in. She was as surprised as an android could be that they had company. "Hello," D7 said. "I am the mother. My name is Ann Droid. Meet to pleased you." *Rewind . . . reverse order.* "Pleased to meet you."

"It's okay, D7," Louie said. "They know."

"Then we must erase all their memories. I suggest we start with those just before birth, and go until those they will have by the time they're twenty-one, just to be sure." A drawer slid open in her back and she pulled out what looked like a remote control.

"And they're willing to help," Terri added.

"In that case . . ." D7 carefully returned her memory eraser to her back drawer. "As I said, meet to . . . pleased to meet you."

D7 shook hands with everyone and removed her wig. "I'm glad that you know. This wig was giving me a cranial-circuitry ache like you wouldn't believe."

"Where were you, anyway?" Katherine asked. "You weren't suppose to leave the *Meatloaf* unguarded."

"Oh, I just went over to one of the neighbors'

for something they called coffee. Odd concoction—somewhat stimulating."

"That's the caffeine," Ellie said.

"No." D7 tilted her head as if in thought. "They definitely called it coffee."

Ellie was examining D7 closely. "Your name is D7?"

"She's an android," Louie said.

"You mean she really is a machine?" BB asked.

"Show them," Katherine ordered.

"Oh, all right, but just this once." D7 reached up, removed her head and tossed it to Ellie.

"Oh, yuck!" Ellie screamed, and looked down at the face in her hands.

"What's the matter?" the face said happily. "Didn't you ever want to get *a head* in life?"

Ellie tossed the head to Katherine, who climbed up on a chair and reattached it to D7's body. "So, do you believe us now?"

At the sight of D7 spinning her head around in circles to adjust its fit, all the students answered with a unanimous "Yes!"

"But you must keep it a secret," Louie said. "If the wrong people find out, it could be a disaster."

"He's right," Katherine said. "If anyone changes even the tiniest bit of history, it could change the whole future. We might not even exist if that happens."

"We won't tell anyone," Ellie said very seriously while raising her right hand. "We swear it."

BB, Perry and Joyce raised their right hands and nodded in agreement.

"Nippy." Arlo smiled. "Totally nippy."

"Holy hamburger!" BB suddenly shouted. "Is that time right?" He pointed to a clock above the door.

"Oh, yes," Louie said. "The century might be wrong, but the time is right."

"Then we're late," BB moaned. "That means only one breakfast tomorrow."

"It's only eight-fifty-nine-thirty P.M.," Louie said. "What's your rush?"

"We said we'd be home at nine sharp," Ellie groaned. "My mom is going to ground me until I graduate."

"Don't worry," Katherine said. "D7 will get you home on time."

"Well." Ellie looked at the clock. "She has exactly twenty seconds to do it."

"No problem," D7 said, giving her head one last turn.

"We better move fast," BB warned.

"No," D7 said. "It would be more helpful if

59

you stayed perfectly still." D7 extended her right hand and spread her fingers so that one was pointing directly at each of the students.

Ellie, BB, Perry and Joyce watched as D7 opened a control panel on her belly and pushed a button. They were instantly surrounded by sparkling golden glitter. Then they were gone.

At one moment the students were in a starship watching an android push her belly button. The next moment they were all home.

Ellie materialized in her kitchen. Her mother jumped about two feet into the air when she turned and saw her daughter standing where she hadn't been two seconds before.

"I didn't hear the door," her mom said.

"Mrs. Droid beamed me home, Mom," Ellie said truthfully.

"That's nice, dear." Ellie's mom thought her daughter was kidding. "Now beam yourself over to your homework."

Joyce materialized in her bathtub, which was filling with water for her brother's bath. Perry appeared on his dining-room table, right on top of the chocolate layer cake his mom and dad were saving for their bridge club. BB landed on his couch, right between his sixteen-year-old sister and her boyfriend, who had just sat down to watch a horror movie.

"Oh boy, popcorn!" BB reached for the bowl on the coffee table. "And a movie? Cool."

BB sat back on the couch to enjoy the show. His sister's boyfriend went home.

Seven

Later that night, on the phone, and early the next morning, on their way to school, Ellie and BB came up with a meatloaf plan. It was designed to help their new friends' mission succeed.

"You think it'll work?" BB asked.

"It has to," Ellie said. "The future depends on it."

They were so excited about their plan that they decided to stop by the *Meatloaf* before school. They were disappointed when D7 answered the door and told them that everyone had just left. She also said she was sorry if she had accidentally transported anyone to an awkward location the night before. "It was the best I could do without exact coordinates."

"It was fine," Ellie said, and BB agreed. Had

Perry or Joyce been present, they might have offered another opinion.

"How long ago did you say they left?" BB asked. "Maybe we can still catch up to them."

"Maybe," D7 said. "But you'd better fly."

"You mean, hurry?"

"I mean . . . fly," D7 said. "Want some jet sneakers?"

"Sure!" BB said.

"Uh, no. Thanks anyway." Ellie pulled BB away. "We'll talk to them at school."

"Why didn't we take the jet sneakers?" BB complained as they walked away from the *Meatloaf.* "It would have been awesome."

"I want to get to school in one piece," Ellie said. "You fall down over your own shadow."

"Hey," BB said, defending his boyhood. "That only happened once. And anyway, the dude tripped me."

Ellie and BB hoped to outline their plan before school, but when they approached the building, the bell rang. They knew they'd have to wait until later. In cooking class, Ellie passed Louie a note, which read simply: "Let's do lunch."

Mr. Mueller didn't notice. He was too busy going over all the meatloaf recipes. He loved comparing them to his own. He paused when he came to Arlo's. "Excuse me, Arlo," Mr. Mueller said, "but your recipe seems somewhat unusual."

"How's that?" Arlo asked. "It's a pretty standard formula—I mean recipe."

"It calls for three pounds of meat and four pounds of ketchup." Mr. Mueller read over the recipe to be sure. "What kind of meatloaf is this?"

"Unleaded premium, of course."

Mr. Mueller found that all the Droid kids had turned in recipes containing a similar ketchup-meat balance. "Interesting," he said thoughtfully. "Very interesting."

Later that day, at lunch, BB arranged his food in eating order. He carefully placed a Snickers candy bar first, followed by some Chips Ahoy! cookies, Chee-tos (crunchy), a Fruit Roll-Up (strawberry), a baloney-and-cheese sandwich, a banana, some grapes and finally, a few cut carrots.

"I always eat in *lanoitirtun* order." BB waited for someone to ask what that meant. When no one did, he said, "You know, nutritional order, only backwards."

When no one paid attention, BB dropped the subject.

Ellie explained the plan to Joyce and Perry while they all waited for the Droids to get through the hot-food line.

Meanwhile, at the other end of the cafeteria, the Buttermans slopped something that looked like a cross between beef stew, a science experiment and a medical specimen onto the Droid kids' trays.

"So, no shrimp today?" Bertha gurgled. "Pity."

"Yeah." Beula stirred a big pot of stuff on the stove. "I sure had a taste for shrimp today." She took a big sip of the brew from the stirring spoon. Her face turned fire-engine red, her nostrils flared, her eyes watered, her mole hairs straightened and her stomach turned. "Perfect!" she exclaimed. "Hey, Bertha, next Wednesday's lunch is ready."

Louie, Terri and Arlo headed for the lunch table. They'd all decided that it would be wise for Katherine to stay away from the Buttermans.

"Why do you eat that Butterman-blech?" BB asked. "You should eat healthy stuff like me." He pulled a stale chocolate-covered cherry from his pocket and popped it into his mouth.

"There, that takes care of the fruit group." He gave the banana to Perry and his grapes to Joyce.

"We would bring our own lunches, but believe it or not, even this stuff beats the heck out of the synthosandwich pills we packed for the trip." Terri looked down at the so-called food on her tray. Suddenly a big bubble appeared in the middle of the glop. When it popped, Terri's face was splattered with gick. "Then again . . . maybe it doesn't."

"We gotta get you guys to a grocery store," BB said.

"What's that?" Perry asked.

"*That* brings us to our plan," Ellie said. "Where's Katherine? I think she should hear this."

"Don't worry," Louie said. "She can hear everything we're saying, right Cap—I mean Katherine?"

"Correct, Dr. Kibbleman." A young child's voice boomed through the entire lunchroom.

Everyone, from the Buttermans to Mrs. Bloomberg's first-grade class, turned and stared. Louie and the rest of the people at his table looked around, as if also searching for the source of the voice. After a few moments everyone returned to their meal already in progress.

"Oops," Louie whispered while reaching into his pocket. He pulled out what looked like a baby transistor radio. "I guess I had the communicator turned up a bit too high."

Outside, by the trash bin behind the lunchroom, Katherine paced back and forth like a caged kindergartner. She hated having to listen to what was happening without taking part. First of all, it seemed undignified for a starship captain, no matter how young, to be hiding by the garbage. Second, she wanted to see whom she was hearing. And third, she was hungry. Whenever she missed lunch she always became one cranky little captain.

Louie turned down the volume dial and placed the communicator in the center of the table. "So." He turned to Ellie and BB. "What's your plan?"

"Okay." Ellie began. "First of all, you need the recipe for ketchup, right?"

"Yeah, how do we get that?" Arlo asked.

"Well, the ingredients are right on the bottle."

"For everyone to see?" Arlo sounded surprised. "Boy, you guys sure, weren't ones to keep a top-secret fuel very hush-hush, were you?"

"The real problem seems to be," Ellie continued, "making enough meatloaf in time to fuel the, uh . . . *Meatloaf.*"

"Yeah," BB said. "Without eating any." All this meatloaf talk was making BB hungry for dinner, even though he was only halfway through lunch.

By the trash bin, Katherine muttered to herself, *"Get to the plan."*

"Which gets us to the plan," Ellie said out loud.

Katherine looked around and, seeing no one nearby, turned up the volume on her communicator so that she could hear the conversation more clearly.

Meanwhile, Bertha and Beula were about to make their daily garbage run. More than once, this journey to the trash bin had resulted in their changing the menu for the next day.

"Let's make it a school project," Ellie said at the lunch table. "We can call it Project Ketchup."

Louie was extremely disappointed with the suggestion. "You mean you want us to tell the whole school the whole truth?" Louie shook his head. "It was bad enough that we had to tell you guys what was really going on. If we tell the entire school, there's no telling what effect it will have on the future."

Katherine banged a tiny fist against the trash bin. She knew time was running out.

"What do we look like—beef jerkies?" BB broke his rule and spoke with his mouth full. He swallowed and continued. "You know how Mr. Mueller is so into all those meatloaf recipes? Maybe we can talk him into a contest to see which one is the best."

Louie, Terri and Arlo all raised their hands to

offer objections. Then they slowly lowered them. It was actually a pretty good idea.

"Tell us more," Louie said. "How would it work?"

By the trash bin, Katherine turned up the volume on her communicator one more notch. She loved the concept of Project Ketchup and didn't want to miss a word.

"Did you hear something?" Beula sniffed at the air as she and her sister approached from the other side of the trash bin. She smelled only the usual stench, which always reminded her of Sunday dinners at her grandma's. "I could have sworn I heard a voice."

"You're just hearing things that aren't there," Bertha said, dismissing her sister's concern. "Have you been eating our own cooking again? You know what the doctor said."

"No," Beula whispered. "I know I heard something."

"It's just the beetballs talking," Bertha insisted.

If it was the beetballs talking, both sisters

clearly heard them say, "Tell us more. How would it work?"

As the Buttermans moved in closer, Ellie continued. "Mr. Mueller will love it. Everyone will make their own meatloaf. The only rule would be that you'd have to use certain ingredients."

"Yeah," BB joined in. "Like meat, salt, pepper and—"

"Ketchup!" seven people at a lunch table and one at a trash bin said at the same time.

Outside, Beula turned to Bertha. "What's a meatloaf?"

"It's a beetloaf, only with meat."

"Got it."

Bertha cleaned out her left ear with her right pinky. "I think it's coming from over there." She pointed toward the other side of the trash. "Did you hear that voice?"

"You mean the one that said 'ketchup'?"

"Yes."

"No."

"I think it was the shrimp."

"You goof-goon." Beula laughed. "Shrimp can't talk."

Bertha stared at her sister for a long time.

Finally Beula's face lit up. "You mean *that* shrimp."

"Shhh," Bertha snapped. "Shut your mouth and open your ears."

"Okay." Bertha cleaned out her right ear with her left pinky and listened.

In the lunchroom, the conversation continued. "But wouldn't the school think it was a horrible waste of good food?" Terri asked.

"Spoken like a true grown-up," BB said.

"I am one, you know, but thanks for the compliment anyway."

"It wasn't a compliment," BB said.

"Anyway," Ellie cut in before BB could continue to spout off, "it wouldn't be a waste because we could say we would serve the whole school a nice meatloaf lunch."

"Anything beats the Buttermans' food." Perry added.

"Anything short of poison," Joyce said.

After a moment Perry repeated, "*Anything beats the Buttermans' food.*"

The Buttermans looked at each other and bared their blackened teeth. Their cheeks puffed out, their nostrils flared, the hair on their backs stood straight up on end.

"If those kids serve the school real food for lunch, our goose is as good as cooked," Bertha snarled.

"We got a goose?" Beula asked hungrily.

For her sister's benefit, Bertha became more specific. "If they taste *meat*loaf at school, we'll be fired."

"Oh." Beula thought about the ingredients they used for their beetloaf surprise. She shivered and said, "You're right."

From around the trash bin they heard a young girl's giggle. "Let's get her," Bertha snarled.

"Yeah." Beula smiled . . . then frowned. "Get who?"

"The shrimp."

"You want to go shopping now?"

Bertha again stared at Beula. After another long time Beula's face lit up. "You mean *that* shrimp."

Both Buttermans raced around the bin. They each grabbed Katherine by an arm and screamed one of their favorite words: *"Gotcha!"*

Eight

"Shrimp kebob!" Bertha drooled while tightening her grip on Katherine's right arm.

"No, no, no," Beula said from the left. "I say we make shrimp suey." She held Katherine's left arm with one hand and snatched the communicator with the other.

Katherine struggled against their grips and their cigarette-onion-anchovy breaths.

"Sweet-and-sour shrimp?" Bertha suggested.

"Nah," Beula laughed. "Just sour."

Both cooks expected Katherine to start crying. That was what always happened when they tried to scare a kindergartner into giving up information or candy. It was also their favorite part of the game. The Buttermans became even angrier when Katherine denied them their perverse pleasure.

"Let go of me this instant!" Katherine ordered in her most captainly tone of voice.

"I guess shrimp *can* talk after all," Beula fumed.

"This one better start talking right now," Bertha snapped. "Or else."

Katherine matched Bertha's snap with one of her own. "Or else what?"

"What?" The Buttermans were perplexed. No other kindergartner had ever asked this question. This was the point where they always told them what they wanted to hear and handed over their Skittles.

"I said, or else what?" Katherine demanded.

"Or else . . ." Beula started to give an answer when she realized she didn't have one. "Or else my sister Bertha will do something. Right, Berth?"

"Right, Beul. And let me assure you, Little Miss Potty-Pants, it will be bad, bad, double-horrible-ugly bad if you don't tell us why you and your brat-pack want to meatloaf us out of our jobs."

Katherine looked at Bertha and then at Beula. "I'd love to stay and chat," she said nonchalantly, "but I really don't have the time." She got a whiff of Beula's breath and Bertha's body odor. "Or the stomach."

Katherine tapped the toe of her left sneaker with the heel of her right. A split second later she zoomed off into the cloudless blue sky and was gone.

Before the Buttermans could blink, she drove back down, flew by at four times the speed of sound and grabbed the communicator out of Beula's very sweaty palm.

"Yech," Katherine moaned when she shot back up, up and away, holding the dripping communicator between the tips of her thumb and forefinger. *I'll probably have to boil this thing,* she thought as she turned her jet sneakers in the direction of the *Meatloaf.*

Bertha looked at Beula, who looked back at Bertha. They both stared at the sky, and then back at each other. "Way, *way, WAY* too much paprika," they shouted, and ran.

In the hall outside the lunchroom, Mr. Mueller was doing a little dance. "I love it! What an absolutely wonderful, super, fantastic, totally terrific idea!" Mr. Mueller had, as expected, responded positively to Project Ketchup.

Ellie, BB, Louie and the rest had run into the teacher as they were leaving lunch and decided to tell him the plan right then and there. He seemed almost too delighted and quick to go along with the proposal.

"Let's go clear this with Principal Walters right now." Mr. Mueller giggled. "When it comes to making meatloaf, there's no time to waste."

"You got that right," Arlo said without even a hint of humor.

Mr. Mueller's voice became equally serious. "Let's go."

"That's them!" a near hysterical voice shrieked as soon as the group walked into Principal Walter's office.

Bertha and Beula pointed at Louie, Terri and Arlo. "They're the ones!" Beula screamed. "The shrim—kindergartner is their sister. Suspend them, Principal Walters! Suspend them all, every stinking, rotten, little rug-rat one of them!"

When Principal Walters looked at Beula as if she were some kind of frosted flake, she quickly added, "Please?"

Principal Walters sighed. "Would you kindly sit down?"

Beula sat down.

"In a chair."

Beula got off the floor and sat in a chair.

"Now," Principal Walters said in his most principalish voice. "What is all this about?"

"It's about their sister." Bertha charged into the conversation and pointed a kielbasalike finger at the students. "She was hiding by the trash, and when we politely asked her if we could be of any assistance . . . she flew away."

"Maybe she ran because you somehow frightened her," Principal Walters suggested.

"No, you don't get it," Bertha said loudly. "She didn't run—she flew."

"You know," Beula piped in. "Like this." She jumped up out of the chair and ran around the office with her arms out to simulate flight. *"Whoosh!"* she shouted over and over again as she pretended to fly.

The flight didn't last long—only until a mighty flab of Beula's flesh knocked over a rack of books, which fell onto a water pitcher, which tumbled into Principal Walters's bowling trophy. The award crashed to the floor, sending the little golden bowling ball smashing through the window, down the hill and through a sewer grating.

Beula quickly popped her gum out of her mouth, rolled it into a ball and stuck it on the end of the little bowler's broken arm. She leaned the now baseless trophy against the wall. "There," she said sheepishly. "Good as new."

Principal Walters didn't seem the least bit surprised by what had just taken place. He'd had meetings with the Buttermans before. Once, he'd found himself covered with green ink and raspberry Jell-O. Another time, they'd accidentally set his pants on fire. And then there was the time he ended up in the hospital emergency room having a peach pit removed from his nose. In comparison, this meeting was going smoothly.

"You're telling me that we have a kindergartner in our school who can fly?"

"Yep!" Both Buttermans smiled. They thought the principal finally understood. He would have to do something. No school could tolerate flying kindergartners.

They waited for the good word from Principal Walters. They hoped that the word would be "suspended." Instead they got: "Are you nuts?"

"Who have you been talking to?" Bertha asked quickly.

"Those doctors don't know everything," Beula pleaded her case. "I really was a giraffe in another life. I have the spots to prove it. Want to see?"

"No!" everyone in the room, including Bertha, yelled.

Principal Walters turned to Louie, Terri and Arlo. "I'm really delighted that you're here, so that we can get this thing settled before it leaves the office." Principal Walters's face turned a peachy shade of pink in embarrassment over the question he was about to ask. "Can your sister fly?"

"Fly?" Louie tried to sound shocked and surprised. "You mean, up in the air?"

"Yes, up in the air," Bertha sneered. "Don't try to lie about it. We saw her do it."

"Well." Louie smiled. "If you saw her do it, then of course she can fly. In fact, she's flown to the moons of Mercury and to every corner of the Milky Way."

"See," Bertha said. "They admit it."

"Oh, yes." Louie grinned. "In fact, our sister isn't really a kindergartner, or for that matter even our sister. She's the captain of a great starship and is known throughout the universe for her exploration of the Beta Quadrant."

"All right." Principal Walters stepped in. "Watch your manners, young man. There's no need for sarcasm." He turned to the Buttermans. "I think you can go now. And the next time you see a student fly by . . ."

"Yes?" both Buttermans asked.

"Duck."

"But it's true, it's true, it's true-true-true." The Buttermans looked even uglier when they whined.

"Enough!" Principal Walters had had it. "I never want to hear you make up such nonsense about one of my students again. Got it? Now, goodbye, good luck and get out!"

Bertha and Beula got out of their chairs, stuck their noses into the air and harumphed their way toward the door. As they passed the students, Bertha whispered, "We'll get you for this, my little pigeon droppings. You and your birdbrain sister too."

"Yeah," Beula whispered. "Remember, diaper-breaths, you ain't heard the last from the . . . from the . . ."

"Buttermans." Bertha came to the rescue.

"Yeah, Buttermans!" Beula agreed.

As they left, Arlo stuck out his tongue, put his thumbs up to his ears and wiggled his fingers. When the Buttermans slammed the door, he smiled. "Wow, that was fun. I haven't done that since I was in school."

"What?" Principal Walters asked.

"I meant—since yesterday," Arlo corrected.

Principal Walters used one of his favorite

phrases. He said it whenever he had no idea what was going on. "Oh, I see," he said, and then quickly changed the subject.

"So, I presume you came to my office for a reason." Principal Walters leaned back in his chair and tried to sound as official as possible. "What can I do for you?" After the Buttermans' accusations he was ready to say yes to almost anything the Droid kids wanted.

For the next fifteen minutes the students and Mr. Mueller enthusiastically presented the meatloaf plan. Principal Walters loved it, and Project Ketchup was officially under way.

Nine

The Buttermans stormed down the hall
like angry twin tornadoes. They ran their pointy
nails along the lockers and stomped their feet
with each step. Their faces were bright red and
their eyes were filled with fury. If they had been
cartoon characters, smoke would have been
coming out of their noses and fire out of their
ears. They were not happy campers.

"Principal Walters is a weenie," Beula muttered as she kicked a pencil all the way to the
other end of the hall.

"How dare he take their side?" Bertha bit her
lower lip, hard. "How? How? *How?*"

"Yeah. How-how-how-how-how-how-how?"
Beula looked for something else to kick. Not
finding anything, she kicked herself behind the
left knee with her right foot. It felt good to kick,

but not to be kicked. "Ouch! I have to stop doing that."

"We can't let them get away with it. We *won't* let them get away with it." Bertha paused. "Beula," she said, "you know what this means?"

"What?" Beula rubbed the back of her knee.

"It means this." Bertha spit, growled and belched.

Beula smiled, recognizing the secret Butterman code that meant the battle had begun. She and Bertha had made it up way back in preschool, when the teacher had insisted that they use the bathroom instead of the sandbox for their personal Butterman business. After they were through, that teacher had joined a circus and become a tiger tamer because she wanted a less hazardous profession.

The Buttermans had made up a war chant to go along with the code. It had changed a bit over the years, but the meaning had stayed the same. Beula answered Bertha's spit, growl, belch, with her own. They both started to chant as they turned left and headed for the lunch-room.

> *"They say we're creeps and nasty,*
> *ugly, cruel and mean.*

Bullies, punks, thugs, monsters
and all things in between.
Evil, no good, tasteless,
and not just in our food.
Crud-buckets, crooks and cranky,
ill-mannered and so rude.
Well, here's what we say to people:
We're ready for a fight.
Think you should be scared of us?
Yeah, dork-dip . . . you're right!"

They spit, they growled, they belched.

"We're Buttermans."

Spit-growl-belch.

"The Buttermans."

Spit-growl-belch.

"We're bad."

Spit-growl-belch.

"So bad!"

Spit-belch-belch-belch-growl-growl-spit.

Bertha and Beula slapped high fives and "accidentally" pushed two second-graders into their lockers. After apologizing, they "accidentally" did it again. The Buttermans felt great. They were ready for war.

"Wow! You mean all this food is real?" Louie looked around in disbelief. As soon as he, Katherine, Arlo and Terri had followed their new friends into the grocery store later that afternoon, they went into a historic state of shock.

Ann Droid picked up a cantaloupe and gave it a squeeze. The melon exploded, covering Ann from headlights to toe circuits with gushy glops of orangy goo. "Yes," she stated. "It is real."

"Sure it's all real," BB said. "Don't you have supermarkets in the future?"

"No," Katherine said, investigating a bunch of bananas.

"Then what do you eat?" Ellie asked.

"Mostly nutrition pills or wafers," Louie said.

"You mean like vanilla wafers?" BB smiled. He loved vanilla wafers.

"Yes, there are vanilla wafers," Louie said as he stuck his finger into a watermelon. "But my personal favorites are liver-and-onion wafers, with a side pill of mashed potatoes."

As the group walked slowly through the store, Louie still couldn't believe that this food was food and not just holographic images in some museum. He opened a jar of nondairy coffee creamer and poured half the contents into his mouth. He then coughed out a milky cloud, which briefly obscured aisle four from view.

"Oh, yeah, it's real all right," Louie said when he stopped coughing. "And quite tasty."

Principal Walters had given the group the go-ahead—and money from the school's cooking budget—to buy the ingredients for a test batch of meatloaf. The plan was falling into place. Ellie and BB suggested using a test batch to fuel the starship, leaving the real batch to feed the school and cover their tracks.

Mr. Mueller had wanted to go to the store, but Principal Walters said the students could go alone. He felt he had to do something to prove he trusted the students. After all, he had just asked some of them if their sister could fly.

The supermarket explorers traveled from aisle to aisle, losing a couple of members of the group along the way. BB stopped by the cookies. "I'll catch up with you," he called while checking out his favorite chocolate chips. "I have to see how my friends are doing."

Ann Droid came to a squealing halt near a display of motor oil and fuses in the houseware-and-hardware aisle. "Yum!" she squeaked. "Now *this* is eating."

Ellie's, Joyce's and Perry's chins dropped when Ann Droid popped open a can of 10W30 and drank the contents in one gulp. As she reached for another, the group heard a tiny mechanical burp.

"Excuse me," Ann apologized, and drained the second can down the sleeve of her dress.

"You'll have to forgive D7." Katherine led the group around the end of the aisle. "She just can't resist snacking between oil changes."

"You know," Ellie said, "we're going to have to pay for that oil."

"Pay?" Terri seemed to be having a bit of trouble with the concept. "With what?"

Joyce snapped her fingers. "I know!" she exclaimed. "How's about money?" She pulled the bills Principal Walters had given them out of the right front pocket of her jeans. "You know . . . this stuff."

"That's money?" Arlo smiled.

"What did you think it was?"

"Kleenex was my guess—" Arlo shrugged.

"You must understand," Louie interrupted. "In the future, paper or metal money is something from the very distant past."

"Full alert! Full alert!" Katherine suddenly ordered, bringing the conversation to an abrupt halt. She pulled out her phaser.

"Look!" She pointed above aisle 7. "I think we're close. Phasers on STUN, just in case we have to fight our way in."

Everyone looked where she was pointing. They saw a dangling sign waving gently in the air-conditioned air. It read:

AISLE 7
SALAD DRESSING
OLIVES
PICKLES
KETCHUP

Before Ellie, Joyce and Perry could say a word, Katherine and the crew tore around the corner, phasers at the ready. A middle-aged couple, who had been trying to decide between kosher dills and gherkins, almost dropped their pickles.

"Sorry, folks." Convinced that this couple

would pose no opposition, Katherine reholstered her phaser. "You can move along now. There's nothing to see. We don't want any trouble. We're just here for the ketchup."

"Kids!" the woman huffed while placing all her pickles in one basket.

"I blame TV," the man said. "Too much of that *Space Trek* or *Star Peck* or whatever that is."

"Really," the woman concurred. "I mean, where is their mother?"

Just then, D7 came strolling around the end of the aisle. As she did, she poured another can of motor oil down the back of her dress. When she noticed the couple staring, she dropped the can and kicked it away. "Hi, kids," she called out in an attempt to normalize the situation and sound motherish. "Remember to eat your peas on the cob."

The couple quickly abandoned their pickles and walked out of the store.

None of the time travelers were paying much attention to anything but the salvation of the future. They were dumbfounded by the unimaginable beauty they now beheld. Row after row of squeeze bottles, glass bottles and even those tiny travel packets of ketchup. Bottle after bottle of pure power. Twelve ounces. Twenty-four ounces. Sixty-four ounces! It was almost too much for them to bear.

Louie picked up the bottle nearest him and sighed heavily. He looked down at what was now in his hands. "It's a miracle."

"It's Heinz," Ellie said, taking the bottle and placing it in their shopping cart. "And I think you all better get yourselves together before someone calls the police."

Ellie gestured with her eyes toward the small crowds that had gathered at either end of the aisle. They seemed particularly interested in Arlo.

"What's the matter with you people?" Arlo cried out. "Haven't you ever seen anyone hug ketchup before?"

Arlo tightly held several big bottles of ketchup to his chest, and actually kissed the top of one.

"You'll have to excuse my son." D7 took the bottles from Arlo, who struggled violently before giving them up. "He just loves his ketchup."

When the crowds continued to stare, D7 remembered what she'd heard the human woman say just before she'd gotten to the ketchup aisle. D7 shrugged her shoulders, sighed and said, "Kids!"

This seemed to satisfy the grown-ups' curiosity, and the ugly crowds broke up into unattractive individual shoppers. It was a good thing too, because a moment later D7 sprang a rather embarrassing oil leak and had to run out of the store at full android speed.

It took the student shoppers only fifteen minutes to finish their job and follow D7's trail of oil spots home. Everyone agreed that they all needed a very good night's sleep. The next day promised to be a meatloaf-making madhouse.

Ten

"Do you think you bought enough ketchup?" Mr. Mueller stared down at the 274 bottles of ketchup the Droid kids and Ellie and company deposited on his desk the next morning.

"It should be sufficient for the test batch," little Katherine said.

Principal Walters had agreed to let Katherine take part in Project Ketchup to further make up for the accusation about flying. He didn't want any lawsuits.

"Plus," Katherine continued. "It was all they had in their fuel reserve stockpile."

Mr. Mueller didn't say a word. He wasn't sure if the Droid kids were up to something he should know about, or if they were just plain, old-fashioned weird. Everything depended on the answer to that question. But Mr. Mueller would have to wait. For now, there was meatloaf to make, and he was as anxious as the kids to get moving.

"Ready?" he called out.

"Aim!" he instructed.

"Cook!" he commanded.

Moments later the meatloaf really hit the fan, as well as the ceiling, desks, blackboard and windows. Ingredients flew like spaghetti in a hurricane as everyone mixed, poured, chopped, broke, crumbled and crunched the makings into meatloaves.

While almost all the recipes contained ketchup in varying quantities, Ellie and BB convinced their classmates that the more ketchupy the meatloaf, the better the grade.

"It's true," Ellie told a skeptical Doreen McAllister. "Mr. Mueller does this meatloaf thing every year, and he always gives extra credit for extra ketchup. My sister said that when she had him, he graded by the ounce."

Doreen grabbed a sixty-four ounce bottle and headed for her chopping block.

"I hear one kid didn't use any ketchup at all, and Mr. Mueller flunked him," BB told Carl Mankiwitz. "The poor guy had to take cooking in summer school . . . and wear an apron with bunnies on it."

Carl grabbed two forty-eight ounce bottles and emptied them into his mixing bowl.

"Sometimes in life you just have to stop and smell the ketchup . . ." Arlo paused and put an open bottle up to his nose. He breathed in and sighed heavily.

"I love it." Louie grabbed the bottle and took a whiff. The sweet aroma brought back great memories of when he and his dad would fill up their star–station wagon with synthochup before going fishing on Feranious 7.

Katherine and Terri sniffed and also remembered. BB sniffed and just got hungry.

Over the next half hour everyone sculpted their meat into loaves. Thanks to Ellie and BB, they all used extra ketchup, which would dramatically increase the years per loaf that the starship would get on the return journey to the future.

"This is great," Louie whispered to Ellie. "It couldn't be going any better."

Louie was right . . . so far.

"What are those snail-lickers doing in there?" Beula huffed, puffed and tried to keep her balance.

"*Shhh!*" Bertha ordered. "You move around

too much when you talk.'' Bertha stood precariously, with one foot sinking into the flab on each of her sister's shoulders. ''I still can't see,'' she hissed down at Beula. She cursed the fact that cooking was taught on the second floor. ''Get up on your toes. You know, like back in ballet class.''

Bertha and Beula had been the stars of their ballet recital. They had scared all the other students into quitting the class by showing them their own version of first and second positions. First was a balled-up fist. Second was that same fist traveling quickly toward the person's nose.

Beula smiled at the memory and grunted her way up onto her toes. Slowly Bertha's eyes rose over the ledge and she briefly peered into Mr. Mueller's classroom. Then, just as in ballet, both sisters heard Beula's toes crack, and they started to fall backward.

At the recital, they had tripped off the stage and landed on the pianist, who ended up spending six months in traction and years trying to overcome his fear of toe shoes, tights and falling tutus. This time Beula landed safely on the damp grass.

''At least we didn't break anything or anyone this time,'' Beula laughed. ''I think our luck is changing.''

Beula heard her sister moan and suggest that perhaps she should think again.

The grass that Beula had landed on was a thin strip of turf that separated the school from the parking lot. Bertha had flown over it and landed on the roof of Principal Walters's car. Just that week, Principal Walters had taken delivery of a shiny, new, red convertible. It was the car he had always dreamed of. But now the principal was in for a rude awakening.

The canvas top proved no match for Bertha's girth, and she tore straight through, ending up with her head under the brake pedal and her bottom sticking up through the gaping wound in the roof.

"You think he'll notice?" Beula said, pulling her sister out of the principal's car.

Bertha stood back and stared at the tattered roof, the bent steering wheel and the snapped-off headrest. "Maybe not," she said hopefully, trying to smooth out the teeth marks in the dashboard. "Maybe not."

In the classroom, the baking of the meatloaf had just begun. When the final temperature control had been set and oven door secured, the bell rang.

"Remember," Mr. Mueller said. "We all meet back here right after school for a meatloaf taste test."

"Do you think it will be refined by then?" Arlo asked.

"What did you say?" Mr. Mueller said, his eyebrows rising almost to his hairline.

"He said will it be *baked* by then," Louie said quickly. "Right, Arlo?"

"Uh, right!" Arlo said. He turned and headed for the door. All the other students quickly followed.

"Don't be late," Mr. Mueller called out over the sound of the exiting students. "I bet these are going to be the best meatloaves ever."

As they walked out of the classroom, the eight participants in Project Ketchup were all gloats and giggles.

"We did it," they all whispered excitedly to each other. "We really did it!"

"They did it! They really did it!" Bertha wheezed and wobbled as she and her sister ran from the damage they had just done. She smelled the meatloaves baking. To her, it was the smell of defeat.

"Who did what?" Beula coughed, choked,

battled for breath and wished she could light up her next cigarette.

"The junior slug-slurpers cooked."

"They didn't."

"They did."

"They're dead."

The Buttermans spent the next couple of hours hiding in the school's boiler room trying to catch their breaths. When they finally did, they headed directly for Mr. Mueller's cooking classroom.

Exactly two hours later, Mr. Mueller hummed Elvis songs and removed the meatloaves from the ovens. His students would be returning shortly, and he wanted everything to be just right.

"This is wrong, wrong, wrong. *R-o-n-g* wrong," Beula gurgled. She peeked through the classroom door, which had been left open a crack to air out the room. "Mr. *Mule*-er is back early."

"Not to worry, O sweet sister of mine," Bertha assured Beula. "I've taken care of everything."

"But-but-but-but-but-but-but—"

"Buttermans' dishonor," Bertha cut in. She clamped her hand over her sister's mouth. "Now, say *three*."

"Three," Beula repeated.

"*Two.*"

"Two."

"*One.*"

"One."

"Paging Mr. Mueller." A voice came over the school's PA system. "Mr. Mueller, you have a parent phone call. Please come to the office."

"Wow! What a coincidence." Beula sounded shocked. "For a parent to call now. Who'd believe it?"

"That's no coincidence." Bertha pulled Beula over to the far side of the door. "That's Cousin Brenda."

"You mean they let her out?"

"Yeah, the warden convinced the judge that keeping her in prison was cruel and unusual punishment."

"For Brenda?"

"No, for the warden." Bertha smiled. She had always liked Cousin Brenda. "I thought we might need some help getting old maggot-mouth Mueller out of the way."

"I still say it's a coincidence," Beula insisted.

"I mean, I didn't know Brenda had a kid in this school."

Before Bertha could either punch some sense into her sister or just punch her senseless, the classroom door swung open. The Buttermans leaned back against the lockers to the right of the door. Mr. Mueller strode out and turned left toward the office.

When he was a safe distance away, the Buttermans scurried into the classroom and locked the door behind them.

Mr. Mueller was perplexed by the call from a woman who put him on hold as soon as he answered the phone. After ten minutes he hung up and headed back to his classroom. He found all his students waiting for him in the hall.

"You could have waited inside," he said, although secretly he was glad he'd be able to see the reactions of the students, particularly the new students, when they saw the meatloaves.

"No, we couldn't," BB said. "The door's locked."

"I didn't lock it."

"Well, someone did. Look." BB tried to turn the doorknob, but it wouldn't budge.

Suddenly BB let go of the knob as if it had

been hit by lightning. Everyone moved away from the door. They all heard the unmistakable noise of spitting, growling and belching, followed by evil-sounding laughter.

"Should we call an exorcist?" Ellie said, half joking.

Mr. Mueller had heard those noises before. "It's the Buttermans," he said.

"So you're saying we *should* call an exorcist?" Ellie asked seriously.

Mr. Mueller reached into his pocket and pulled out his key. A moment later he turned the handle and threw open the door. Everyone gasped. There were the Buttermans rolling around on their bloated bellies in a sea of empty meatloaf pans and roasting pots.

Beula held up a small piece of meatloaf between her thumb and forefinger. She flicked it at Katherine, who caught it and put it in her pocket.

"Where's the rest of the meatloaf?" Katherine demanded.

"As a matter of fact, Miss Snotty Pants," Bertha said as she picked her teeth with a matchbook cover, "that was the last piece. We ate the rest."

"Yeah." Beula let out a belch that shook the beakers in the science room downstairs. "They were deeeeeeeeeeeeeeeeeeeee-licious."

"And—and—and—and—and the leftover ketchup?" Louie fearfully stammered.

"What's meatloaf without gobs of ketchup?" Beula wiped what Louie had hoped was lipstick from her lips. "Ketchup is our favorite continent."

"You mean condiment," Bertha corrected.

"Where's a mint?" Beula looked angrily at the students, hoping to spot the one sneaking mints without paying the usual candy toll of half the box, bar or bag.

"There are no mints, you idiot," Bertha snapped. "But there's still half a bottle of ketchup left." She held up a half-full forty-eight-ouncer and waved it in front of Beula.

"Yum." Beula drooled.

"Noooooo!" eight students and one teacher pleaded.

"Yes. Oh, yes, yes, yes!" Beula stuck her ketchup-coated tongue out at the students. "Dibs on licking the cap."

"Come, sweet sister," Bertha said. "Let us retire to the privacy of our lunchroom so that we can truly enjoy the last of the ketchup."

As the Buttermans left, laughing, Louie, Katherine, Arlo, Terri and Mr. Mueller started to cry.

Eleven

The Buttermans danced. The Buttermans skipped. The Buttermans jumped. The school shook, causing what a TV newscaster later described as "minor damage, probably the result of a small and extremely localized earthquake."

Bertha held the last half-full bottle of ketchup to her lips and waited for the sweet red stuff to ooze down the spout. When it finally made it to the rim, Beula grabbed the bottle and quickly sucked out its contents.

"Yep," she said, wiping ketchup from her chin with her sleeve. "Definitely my favorite continent."

"You selfish pig." Bertha squinted at her sister.

"Why, thank you, dearie!" Beula momentarily got her tongue caught in the bottle, where it was searching for any remaining ketchup. "From the number of meatloaves you wolfed down, I'd say that you're quite the oinkity-oink-oinker yourself."

The two sisters then *oink-oinked* their way around the lunchroom to celebrate their victory.

"What do we do now?" Louie stomped his feet.

"No fair! No fair! No fair!" Arlo, Terri and Katherine cried out in a chorus.

Ellie, who had two very whiny younger brothers and was therefore accustomed to tantrum control, stepped forward to settle everyone down. "Would you guys grow up? We have a problem and we have to do something about it. Acting like babies won't help you save your world."

"Babies?" Katherine frowned. "Don't call me a baby. I have a kid your age!" the kindergartner huffed.

"What?" Mr. Mueller said, straightening up from checking each pot and pan to see if the Buttermans had missed a loaf—which they hadn't.

"I mean," Katherine quickly said, "I mean, I have a *brother* your age. Right, Louie, Arlo, Terri?"

"Right." The three nodded vigorously.

"Yeah. Sorry, Mr. Mueller," Ellie piped up. "We're just sad because we wanted Project Ketchup to work."

"Same here." Mr. Mueller sighed. "I guess we'll have to do a new test batch on Monday."

Suddenly Katherine's Bozo the Clown belt buckle started beeping. Before Mr. Mueller noticed, she quickly pushed down on Bozo's nose and asked if she could be excused to go to the bathroom.

Moments later she ran back into the classroom and panted, "Mr. Mueller, what do you think about working on weekends?"

In the lunchroom, the Buttermans stopped celebrating.

"What if those little punk-ernickels rise up and bake again?"

Bertha scratched each of her chins, momentarily getting a pinky caught between the third and fourth folds.

"Then we eat again?" Beula felt a sharp gas pain of protest shoot across her stomach. She punched herself right below the belly button to teach herself a lesson. "Shut up," she screamed at her beltline. "You'll eat when and what I tell you to eat."

The gas pain tripled in intensity, and Beula doubled over in agony.

Bertha grabbed her sister by the thinning hair on the top of her head and dragged her toward the door. "Come on, Beula. No time to play. We've got work to do."

Mr. Mueller was happy to go along with a Saturday bakefest, and Principal Walters was quick to agree. He approved the request the moment he heard that the Buttermans had devoured the first batch of meatloaf. It also didn't hurt the cause when Katherine sweetly said, "Is it true that they said I can fly? How silly. I'm not even in a grade yet. My mommy and daddy are gonna be real, real mad."

"Nobody wants that," Principal Walters said as he quickly ushered the group out of his office. "Happy meatloaf making." He beat a hasty retreat, closing his door behind him.

Mr. Mueller dismissed his students outside of Principal Walters's office. "Everyone meet at the classroom at nine tomorrow morning. If you have previous plans and can't make it, it won't go against your grade."

As the class dispersed, the eight ketchup conspirators walked down the hall. Ellie turned to Katherine.

"What happened with your beeper?" she asked.

"I have a communicator," Katherine said snootily. "Starship captains do not have *beepers.*"

"Whatever." Ellie hated being corrected by a grown-up, particularly a five-year-old grown-up. "So? Are you going to share the secrets of your *communicator* message or not?"

"Shhh." Katherine looked up and down the hall to make sure they were alone. Ellie also hated being shushed by anyone.

Katherine signaled for everyone to gather around her by a large trash can near the end of the hall. The can had once had the words PITCH IT! printed on its side, but someone had crossed out the *P*. BB always found it very amusing to stand by the sign and scratch his belly until someone asked him what he was doing. Then he'd point to the sign and say that it was his way of helping the environment.

Today, however, BB was not in a joking mood. When everyone was in a huddle around the can, Katherine held up her little hand for silence and started whispering.

"It was D7 on the emergency communicator priority one channel. She said we are in big, big trouble. We stand at yellow alert."

"What's the problem?" Louie asked.

"While D7 was monitoring the time-displacement core, she noted a small but definite ripple in the space-time continuum."

Louie, Terri and Arlo gasped. "What does that mean?" Ellie, Joyce, BB and Perry all asked.

"That," Katherine said, "means that we have less than twenty-four hours before the time porthole closes and we never make it home. We'll be trapped in this century forever." She paused and swallowed hard before continuing. "If we don't fuel the starship and leave tomorrow . . . the future, as we know it, is past."

"For real?" BB asked.

"For positive sure real," Arlo answered.

No one said a word for a moment, until Katherine took command. "Come on." She motioned with her right arm. "Let's go to the *Meatloaf.* We have some serious planning to do."

As the group moved away from the trash can, Ellie silently forgave Katherine for shushing her.

Before the group made it to the end of the hall, the lid of the trash can mysteriously started to rise. Two beady sets of eyes peered out. Then twenty fat, sweaty fingers emerged over the rim.

"They *are* space monsters." Beula pushed the lid open all the way and tried to stand up. "Told you so."

"Quick," Bertha ordered. "Follow those space geeks."

Bertha also tried to stand up, but the sisters' flesh filled the trash can so tightly that they couldn't budge.

"We're losing them!" Beula struggled against her sister's flab.

"Okay." Bertha had a plan. "On the count of three . . . push to the right. One . . . two . . . three!"

Both sisters threw their mighty weight to the right. The trash can tipped over and started rolling down the hall. It continued to pick up speed until it smashed through the door and out onto the street. The can stayed on a roll until it reached the intersection of Hayes and Sutton roads. There it tumbled into the path of an oncoming garbage truck. The driver tried to swerve, but he hit the bottom end of the can, causing the Buttermans to pop out like champagne corks on New Year's Eve.

Bertha and Beula flew twenty feet and bounced ten more before coming in for a flubby landing. They left two long greasy skid marks on the concrete before slamming into the curb. They quickly jumped up and lumbered off. The truck's crew was amazed. In all their years on the job, they had never seen so much garbage run so fast.

As the sisters headed down the street, Beula pulled a piece of chewed gum out of her hair. A first-grader had tossed it into the trash can on his way out of school. Beula looked at it carefully before popping it into her mouth.

"Yum." She chomped. "Peppermint . . . I think."

"Quiet, beans-for-brains," Bertha snapped. "Remember, we've got a job to do."

"You mean like making next Friday's lunch?"

"No. I mean like stopping those moongoons."

Bertha stopped running, which, with her

weight and resulting momentum, took half a block. Beula employed her usual method of stopping. She fell down.

Bertha pointed. About a hundred yards ahead, a group of eight students walked slowly down the street.

"Now shut up, bat-breath," Bertha snarled to her sister through gritted teeth. "And follow those aliens."

Twelve

The Buttermans hid behind trees, mail-boxes and the occasional bus as they followed their prey around corners, through the park and up a small hill. They were surprised when the group turned up a short walkway that led to a very earthly- and ordinary-looking ranch house.

"That doesn't look like a UFO to me." Beula shook her head. "I ain't never heard of a brick flying saucer . . . with shutters."

The Buttermans were about to give up the chase when the students walked to the door. Bertha and Beula Butterman watched as the flying kindergartner, Katherine, opened the screen. They heard a loud hissing sound and saw a puff of smoke. Several silver stairs appeared out of thin air.

"Did you see that?" Beula poked Bertha.

"Do you feel this?" Bertha punched Beula.

"Yes," Bertha whispered.

The Buttermans couldn't believe the scene that was unfolding before them. The students walked up the steps and vanished. The smoke and the hissing sound returned when the screen door automatically closed.

"We must be in the Bermuda Rectangle." Beula's voice quavered slightly.

"Triangle," Bertha corrected.

"Try what angle?" Beula asked without taking her eyes off the house. "I'm telling you, that place gives me the wigglies. I even got moose bumps. Look."

Bertha was about to correct her sister again, but when she looked at the bumps on Beula's arm, the term *moose* bumps did seem somehow more appropriate.

"I want a closer look." Bertha stared at the mysterious screen door.

Beula put her arm up against her sister's nose.

"At the house, you skin-rash. Not at your arm."

Beula was disappointed. She found her arms, and their moose bumps, quite interesting. "Your loss," she snarled under her breath. The two sisters crept toward the brick spaceship with the white picket fence.

Intruder alert! Intruder alert! The words appeared on D7's forehead. A siren sounded from her belly button, and her ears flashed bright red. D7 had tied her circuits directly into the ship's security system so that she could constantly monitor the area. D7's nose began to whistle, and her head started spinning around on her shoulders. She tried to talk but kept getting in her own way.

"Would . . ."

INTRUDER . . .

". . . somebody . . ."

ALERT!

". . . please . . ."

INTRUDER . . .

". . . turn . . ."

ALERT . . .

". . . me . . ."

INTRUDER . . .

". . . off?"

Terri ran up and yanked the android's right pinky. The security system disengaged.

"Thanks," D7 said. "That was making me a little dizzy."

"I bet," Terri said, gently turning D7's head around so that her face was once again on the same side as her toes.

"What did all that Alert stuff mean?" BB asked.

"It means," Katherine said, running to a control panel, "that we have company."

Outside the *Meatloaf,* the unexpected guests had set off every sensor in the book. As soon as the Buttermans walked through the gate, they broke the force field that D7 had made to look like a picket fence. They also triggered the heat, movement, and particularly the smell sensors.

The savage sisters skulked their way toward the house. When they thought they heard something from inside, they ducked behind what they thought was a tree. That lasted until Beula tried to lean against it and fell directly through. She ended up bottom down on the ground.

"That tree," Beula said shakily. "I think it moved."

"No. Look," Bertha said. "It ain't a real living tree at all." Bertha ran her hand back and forth through the trunk. It passed through as if it were going through smoke.

"It ain't alive?" Beula said.

"Nope."

"Then it's a ghost tree!" Beula shrieked loudly. She struggled to her feet and tried to run, but Bertha grabbed her by the flapping roll of flab at the back of her neck.

"It's no ghost tree." Bertha tossed her sister back down to the ground. "It's one of those holo-whatchamacallit doohickey thingies."

"Ohhhhh." Beula looked up at her sister with pride. She loved it when Bertha used technical, scientific terms. "You are *so* smart."

"Watch and marvel." Bertha walked right inside the tree and stopped. The image remained, making her look as if she were half birch and half Butterman.

"See?" She stepped out of the tree. "It's a fake."

"Who do those little snot-puppets think they're dealing with?" Beula snorted. "They can't fool a Butterman."

"Let's see what they're up to." Bertha moved closer to the *Meatloaf,* with Beula less than a step behind.

In the starship, Katherine, Arlo, Terri and Louie took their battle stations. As directed, Ellie, BB, Joyce and Perry took cover.

"I have two radar pulses moving in slowly. Range: twenty feet."

Arlo's voice shook with fear. "What are those things?" he shouted. "They're huge! Enormous! They're going to crush us. They're . . ."

"The Buttermans." Terri had established visual contact. It was not a pretty picture.

The Buttermans flattened themselves, as much as possible, against the house. Beula pressed and rubbed her back against what she thought would be rough, perfect-for-back-scratchin' bricks. She rubbed as hard as she could, determined to get rid of a seven-year itch that had taken up residence between her shoulder blades. But instead of getting relief, she slid along the smooth metal shell of the *Meatloaf*. She crashed into her sister and stomped on her foot.

While Bertha yowled, Beula complained, "Hey, those bricks are smooth and made of metal."

"Then they ain't bricks, you blockhead." Bertha moaned in agony, convinced that the three middle toes on her left foot were now about as thick as an unrolled Fruit Roll-Up.

"Then what are they?"

"They're . . . space-people stuff."

Again, Bertha's use of technical language made Beula smile. "How'd you get so smart?"

"Don't know." Bertha started to get back the feeling in two toes. "I guess I just got the brains in the family."

Beula twirled her mole hairs and sighed. "And I had to settle for the looks."

"Come on." Bertha shook her foot and changed the subject. She had always been secretly jealous of Beula's looks. "Let's get down to business."

Beula gave her mole hairs one final twist, causing them to curl in a way that Bertha's never would. "Okay, smart one. Whatever you say."

The Buttermans moved against the wall until they came to a window. Both sisters turned, looked and found themselves face-to-face with several very unhappy . . . baboons.

Moments earlier, inside the *Meatloaf,* Katherine had given the order: "Engage."

"Aye, aye, Captain," D7 said, and beamed the Buttermans away from the starship. BB had suggested the destination for the beam-out, and everyone had happily agreed.

One second the Buttermans had been standing next to the house; the next they were seated on large rubber tires in a huge metal cage. Out of the corner of her eye Bertha read the words: BABOON EXHIBIT. CLOSED FOR RENOVATION.

Several baboons moved toward the intruders, screeching and screaming. The Buttermans turned toward the baboons and did the same. The baboons ran away.

Over the next hour or so, until the zookeepers made their rounds and called the police, Bertha and Beula made the adjustment to a life of captivity. When the police arrived, they were happily picking fleas from two large baboons and waiting for feeding time.

Meanwhile, on the starship, the crew and their compatriots were busy planning the next day's meatloaf making, and the salvation of the future of humankind.

Several hours later, after making bail and stopping back at the zookeeper's office to demand their missed meal, the Buttermans wasted no time getting to the telephone. They called the army, navy, marines, air force, coast guard, postal service, UFO societies, psychic connection fan clubs and Brenda.

"We've got those job-stealing, meatloaf-making space goobers now," Bertha said after the final call. "Tomorrow belongs to the Buttermans."

Thirteen

"This is it, huh?" BB said as he and Ellie walked toward school the next morning. "The whole, like, future depends on what we bake today."

"Uh-huh." For once Ellie didn't have much to say.

A half block later BB said, "What if we blow it?"

"Then we have four new kids at school for good . . . and they're all grown-ups."

"Not cool," BB said, and scratched.

"Not cool at all," Ellie agreed. She fought back an almost overwhelming desire to do some scratching of her own.

While the students walked, the Buttermans were on the warpath. To get into the mood, Bertha thought they should wear war paint and black leather.

"Paint your face and get ready to party," she told her sister.

Bertha painted three large red streaks on one cheek and a huge green X on the other. She put yellow circles on her chins and wrote UFO SMASHER in black-and-white letters on her forehead.

Beula painted her face blue.

Joyce and Perry joined BB and Ellie at the playground. As they walked toward the building, the crew of the *Meatloaf* materialized in their path.

"Don't do that!" BB jumped about a foot into the air.

"Sorry. We figured no one would be around on a Saturday and we could take a more civilized route to school," Louie explained.

The group walked solemnly to Mr. Mueller's classroom. When they got there, the teacher was waiting, ketchup in hand . . . in pockets, in cases and on the tables.

"Wow!" Louie said. "Where did you get all this ketchup?"

"I've been saving up," Mr. Mueller said casually. "For a special occasion." He grinned.

Within minutes the rest of the class arrived. Mr. Mueller took his position at his desk. He looked around at his students and paused dramatically. "Class," he said, "let's bake."

"Let's boogie." The Buttermans spit, growled and belched their way out of their house, into their car and all the way to school.

"Let's move quickly, students," Mr. Mueller said as soon as everyone had taken their places. "There's no time to waste."

"No kidding," Louie whispered to Ellie, who had noticed that Mr. Mueller was staring rather strangely at the group—particularly at the new kids.

"El dude es psychic," BB said, using the opportunity to practice his Spanish.

Arlo and Perry nodded while Katherine just stared back at the teacher. Finally Mr. Mueller looked away and clapped his hands, signaling the start of *Meatloaf Making 2—The Final Batch*.

The students got to work, quickly modeling their ketchup-soaked meat into loaves. Mr. Mueller had arrived at school early and had the onions chopped, the bread soaked, the ketchup bottles opened and every other meatloaf ingredient imaginable lined up and ready to go.

Once every oven was set and the meatloaves were in place on their racks, Mr. Mueller dismissed the class.

"It'll take about two hours before they're done," he said. "You may as well go out and enjoy your Saturday. I'll wait here and take them out. You can try them on Monday. Class dismissed."

"All right!" BB stood up and shouted. He didn't mean to do it. It was just that he always shouted whenever a teacher used the phrase "class dismissed," "No homework" or "I could have sworn I left the test on my desk. I guess you'll have to take it tomorrow."

Once BB caught the stares from seven of his classmates, he quickly sat down while everyone else headed for the door. Moments later only eight students remained in the classroom.

"If you don't mind," Katherine said, "we'd like to wait."

Mr. Mueller smiled.

When Bertha and Beula arrived at school an hour and a half later, they expected to see at least an airborne division, a SWAT team and a couple of mail carriers surrounding the building. Instead, when they pulled into the parking lot, it looked like a Butterman family reunion.

No one except for Cousin Brenda and a few TV talk-show hosts had believed their story. The TV show people had gotten busy searching for others who had contacted, or better yet married, meatloaf-making Martians. Brenda had called the other cousins.

Actually, the cousins didn't really believe the story either, but it didn't matter. With the possibility of free meatloaf and a chance to be mean, no one saw a need to quibble.

Baxter, Bruno, Boris, Betina, Brumhilda and Babs all waved a greeting and asked, "When do we eat?"

"Soon, my sweet cousins, soon." Bertha smiled. "Let's get into the school."

As they moved toward the building, Beula

caught up with her favorite cuz. "Babs, you look terrific. You lost weight!"

Babs fluffed her facial hair and smiled a toothless grin. "Do you really think so?" She continued to walk, causing the concrete to crack beneath her feet with each step.

"Definitely," Beula said. "Look at how small the cracks are compared to last year."

"You might be right." Babs blushed. "I do feel lighter on my feet."

It took the Buttermans almost twenty minutes to get through the doors and up the steps to the second floor. By then the meatloaves were ready to come out of the ovens.

Carefully the students and Mr. Mueller removed the hot pans and lined them up on a long, narrow metal table near a window to cool. Mr. Mueller opened the window to speed up the process.

"You know," Mr. Mueller said, "I think this batch is even better than the first."

BB and Ellie shook hands with Arlo and Terri. "Good job, sports." BB tried to sound snooty. "Yes indeedily-deedily-do."

While this was going on, Katherine secretly pushed a long, thin power guage into one of the loaves and looked at the readings.

"This batch *is* better." She nodded her head. "Much more ketchup."

"Now only one question remains." Mr. Mueller scratched his chin. "Where are we going to keep all this meatloaf until Monday?"

No one wanted to answer too quickly and arouse any suspicions. After about ten seconds Louie snapped his fingers. "I know. We have plenty of room at our house."

"I was hoping you'd say that." Mr. Mueller smiled. "Now there's something I'd like to say to you."

Before Mr. Mueller could have his say, the door burst open and the Buttermans stampeded through. Their nostrils flared and there was a wild look in their eyes. The smell of meatloaf was strong.

"We got you now," Bertha snarled. "You want to make things easy on yourselves and confess that you're UFO beastie creatures? Or do you want to talk to my cousins?" Bertha pointed with her thumbs to the Buttermans spread out on either side of her, blocking not only the path to, but also the view of, the door.

Brenda Butterman stepped forward, cracked all her knuckles and belched her best belch.

"What an amateur," BB scoffed. He swallowed and let out a burp to beat the Butterman.

Brenda was genuinely impressed. She put a heavy arm around BB's shoulder. "Very nice. We must get together and share techniques."

"Have your people call my people," BB said, trying to duck away. "We'll meet and eat."

"Wonderful," Brenda said, gripping him harder. "But tell me now, if you will, when you burp after a meal, do you first have to swall—"

"Enough shop talk!" Bertha pulled Brenda's arm off BB. "We have aliens to unmask and meatloaf to eat."

"Sorry," Brenda said to BB with a shrug. "Duty calls."

"I understand," BB said.

The two returned to their respective groups just as a crackling noise and a metallic sounding voice filled the room. "Emergency! Ketchup channel red. Repeat: Ketchup channel red!"

D7 felt she had no choice but to go to ketchup channel red, which broadcast out loud, even if the crew's communicators were turned off. Using it meant that the situation had gotten so bad that there was no longer time to keep secrets or hide identities.

"The space-time continuum is in ripple flux one," D7 stated rapidly. "Estimated porthole collapse in seventeen minutes, forty-two seconds. Delta-bravo-alpha-bet-soup." The last line was a code that showed the message was for absolute real and that this was not a test.

"We'll take those, thank you very much." Bertha yanked Katherine's communicator off her belt. Beula, Bruno and Babs did the same to Louie, Arlo and Terri.

The starship crew tried to grab them back, but the four Buttermans tossed the communicators to four other Buttermans, three of whom crushed them in their pawlike hands. Only Baxter avoided the temptation to crush the precious device. Instead, he bit it cleanly in two.

"See," Bertha said proudly to her cousins, "I told you they're space monsters."

"Yeah." Beula was starting to drool uncontrollably. "Monsters with meatloaves."

Without the communicators there was no way D7 could lock onto the crew's coordinates for emergency beam-out. But escape was the second most pressing issue at the moment. The first lay cooling on a metal table by an open window at the far side of the room.

While each Butterman found it mildly interesting that they were in the presence of suspected extraterrestrials, they found the fact that they were in the same room with twenty fresh-baked meatloaves to be the crowning achievement of their lives. That feeling was verified when Bertha looked dreamily at her cousins and whispered those two little words that meant everything to a Butterman: "Let's eat."

Like wolves on a kill, sharks in a frenzy or shoppers at a sale, the Buttermans charged the meatloaves.

"Stop!" Katherine shouted, but it was like screaming at a hurricane to settle down or yelling at a tidal wave to cool it.

Only one person could stand in their way. There was only one final hope for the future of the world. BB pushed between Louie and Joyce. "Move aside," he said. "I need room to work."

BB took a deep breath, clenched his fists, gritted his teeth and headed for the meatloaf. It was no contest. No one had ever beaten BB to the dinner table. He had six brothers and sisters. All of them were skinny. BB reached the meatloaves four steps ahead of the first Butterman. When he got there, he didn't hesitate. He pushed the end of the table against the window and lifted the other end so that all the meatloaves started to slide. One by one they slid out the window and dropped to the ground below. Some smushed onto the cement sidewalk, but most fell safely, pan side down, on the ground.

The Buttermans froze in their tracks. They were angry, disappointed, hurt and *hungry*.

"Uhhh, sorry?" BB said.

His apology was not accepted.

"Get him!" Beula commanded.

All the Buttermans, arms straight out and hands grasping at the air, stormed toward BB.

BB jumped out the window.

"No!" Ellie and the rest screamed.

Mr. Mueller saw his chance and took it. He tried to push the remaining students out the door before the Buttermans could turn around.

"Get out now!" he yelled as they all fell into the hall and he slammed the door behind them. "Get the meatloaves!" Mr. Mueller pushed with all his might, holding the door closed to try to slow down the crush of Buttermans that would inevitably follow.

As the students started to back away, there was a huge bang against the door. The entire frame shook, but Mr. Mueller managed to hold it closed. "Run! Run before the porthole closes!" he shouted.

"Who are you?" Louie asked.

Bang! The door actually started to splinter.

"Run now!"

Boom! The Buttermans were using Babs as a

battering ram. Mr. Mueller wouldn't be able to hold them back for long.

"Let's go!" Katherine finally called. "And, thanks . . . whoever you are." She led the group down the hall.

As they ran, they heard Mr. Mueller shout back, "You're welcome." He paused a second before calling out something Ellie and her friends didn't understand. "Dallas Cowboys: seventeen; New Pluto Patriots: twelve."

"What did that mean?" Ellie ran beside Louie, who looked more than a bit shaken.

"That was a Super Bowl score," Louie said as they headed down the stairs.

"Oh." Ellie was no longer interested. She hated sports.

"Yeah," Louie said just before slamming the handle on the door and heading outside. "The score of Super Bowl MVDCCCXXI . . . in the year 6789."

"Help!" The students and time travelers heard BB before they saw him. When they turned the corner to the cooking-classroom side of the building, they found him hanging by his fingers from the second-floor ledge.

"BB's okay!" Ellie shrieked happily.

"Not for long," BB yelled back. "I'm slipping."

BB could hang on only another second and a half. Then he started to fall. Every candy bar he'd ever eaten passed before his eyes.

While everyone screamed, Katherine tapped the toe of her right sneaker with the heel of her left. She shot into the air and toward BB at jetsneaker speed. She caught up to him when he was halfway to ground zero, grabbed him by the shirt collar and tried to fly up.

Unfortunately, with BB's substantial weight and the limitations of high-top jet sneakers, the best she could do was slow down the fall.

Now they were both falling at a still-dangerous speed. Katherine had no choice. She reached down with one hand and yanked the lace of her left sneaker. This released a sudden and extremely powerful burst of energy.

BB and Katherine came to a midair halt, six inches above the ground, before the sneaker's astrojet soles blew out completely from the strain. The two tumbled safely to earth.

"Yeah!"

"All right!"

"Cool!"

"Frosty!"

Everyone shouted joyously until they again

heard the word "Help!" This time the one doing the screaming was Katherine. "My sneakers are going critical!"

Katherine's sneakers were smoking. A sudden sizzling sound filled the air.

Joyce and Ellie were the closest. They raced to Katherine. When they reached her, they each yanked a sneaker off a foot and tossed it into the empty school parking lot. A second later, both shoes exploded like powerful foot grenades, leaving two size-five potholes in the cement.

BB walked over and gave Katherine a giant bear hug.

"There's no need for that." Katherine wriggled out of his grasp. She saluted Joyce and Ellie for their bravery.

From inside the school, they all heard the sound of wood cracking and breaking apart. Then there was a low rumbling noise that sounded like a stampede of overweight cattle. The rumbling got louder and louder.

Frantically, everyone picked up a couple of meatloaves and put one under each arm. They ran for the starship as fast as they could, knowing that the Buttermans would be close behind.

Fourteen

"Inject meatloaf now!" Katherine ordered.

Simultaneously, BB, Ellie, Joyce, Perry, Louie, Arlo and Terri placed the ends of their meatloaves against tiny crystal tubes that had popped out of a holographic brick near the left front basement window. The tubes had appeared when Katherine pushed a button on the holographic gas meter. Each was about two inches long and about half as wide as a juice-box straw.

As soon as the meatloaves were in place, Katherine pushed another button. There was a gushy, slurpy sound as the meatloaves were pulled from the hands that held them and sucked through the tiny tubes. BB and the rest of the now-a-days bunch jumped back, while

Louie, Terri and Arlo each turned and grabbed another meatloaf.

"Don't worry," Louie said to the somewhat unnerved students. "Self-serve takes some getting used to."

· After all sixteen meatloaves were injected and liquefied, D7 stuck her head out of the kitchen window. "We're up to a little over three-quarters of a tank. That should be more than enough to get home."

The door hissed open. "Come on board," Katherine said to BB, Ellie Joyce and Perry. "I don't think we should say our goodbyes in public."

The Buttermans were delayed only slightly in their chase. After a few minutes of pushing, shoving, punching and pinching, they decided to draw straws for the four meatloaves that had been smushed against the sidewalk and left behind. Bertha, Brenda, Brumhilda and Bruno were the obvious winners. They were the best drawers in the bunch, and had been that way ever since first-grade art class.

It took the four winners only seconds to peel their prizes off the cement, brush off the dirt and an occasional ant, and scarf down the spoils of their victory.

"Now let's get the rest." Bertha spit an onion bit and a piece of an old rubber band from her mouth. "There's no way those aardvark aliens are getting away with our meatloaves."

The Butterman cousins snorted in agreement, and the whole group headed for the starship . . . with their prisoner in tow.

"I wish we could go with you," Ellie said sadly, giving Louie a goodbye hug.

"I wish you could too," Louie said.

"They *can* go with us," D7 said matter-of-factly.

"We can?"

"They can?"

"They can." D7 pulled what looked like four postage stamps from her red-and-white-checkered apron.

"What are those?" BB asked.

Everyone except Katherine moved closer to D7 to get a better look. Katherine was too busy doing the pre–time-travel flight check to pay much attention to D7's tinkerings.

"I call them Mama Droid's time-displacement patches. I worked on them while you were in school. Believe me, with the vacuuming, warp-core maintenance, laundry, beaming you and your friends all over town and just picking up after you guys, it wasn't easy."

Ellie and her friends examined the patches. Each one had a different picture of a smiling D7 and the words STRAIGHT FROM MAMA DROID'S LAB printed on the nonsticky side.

"What do they do?" Ellie asked.

If a machine could be proud, D7 was bursting at the rivets. "All you have to do is peel off the backing and stick a Mama Droid's time-displacement patch on any nonhaired part of the human body. Because of the highly attractive picture, I suggest the forehead."

"And what happens then?" Joyce asked.

"Then the aging or antiaging effects of time travel are blocked via a displacement field. It's created by the stamp's interaction with the electromagnetic forces surrounding the human body. The instructions are right on the stamp."

"D7," Louie said. "You're a genius!"

"No, no, no." D7 turned on her blush program. "I'm only mechanical."

Ellie looked closely at the patch she was holding. "So that means that we could travel with you into the future?"

"Without getting any older along the way," Perry added.

"And now that you have the recipe for ketchup," Joyce said, "you could bring us back to right now."

"Or maybe after next week's math test," BB offered.

"Exactly," D7 said.

"That's great," Louie said, his voice cracking in his excitement. "I can't wait for you to meet my kids."

"This is totally frozen yogurt," Arlo cheered.

"Yeah." Terri jumped in. "The historians will go nutbag nova over a chance to actually speak to—no offense—primitive people."

There was cheering, there was clapping, there was celebrating. Then there was silence. Everyone realized that Katherine had not joined the party. In fact, she hadn't said a word. They all slowly turned and looked in her direction.

The captain was busy checking the ketchup-containment tanks for any leaks or lesions. After a minute or two of being stared at by everyone, including D7, she said matter-of-factly, "Oh all right, but only a short visit."

The celebration was back on, but not for

long. INTRUDER ALERT! INTRUDER ALERT! The words once again appeared on D7's forehead.

"Not again!" D7 moaned just before the siren screeched from her belly button. This time Ellie pulled D7's pinky before her head started to spin.

Everyone ran over to the video monitors, where they saw a long and hungry row of Buttermans, with one captive teacher in the middle, stretched out in front of the *Meatloaf*. Bertha and Beula took a step forward and pulled Mr. Mueller along with them.

"We know you're in there," Bertha called out. "And we know that you can hear us."

"Do we really know those things?" Beula whispered.

"Yes," Bertha hissed.

"Oh, okay." Beula was happy that she knew something that she had no idea she knew. She didn't know why it made her happy to know it, but she knew that it did. Knowing *that* made her happier still.

Beula's mood was broken by Bertha's order to the entire group. "Quick, everyone, hold hands!"

"Hold that order, D7. Repeat: Hold that order!" Captain Asher countermanded the order she had just issued, which was to beam the Buttermans to a bat cave in Brazil.

"What's wrong?" Ellie asked.

"They're holding hands," Louie answered. "If we transported them that way, their molecules would get all mixed together. When they rematerialized, they might just end up as one giant, nine-headed, eighteen-legged, five-thousand pound super-Butterman."

The thought was enough to make everyone in the *Meatloaf* shudder. "Stand by," Katherine said. "I have an idea." She looked at the current-day students. "I think you all need a crash course in starship operations."

"Gotcha! *Gotcha! Gotcha!*" Bertha shouted after realizing that all the Buttermans were still in front of the ranch house and there wasn't a baboon in sight. Bruno *looked* like a baboon, but Bertha could tell that he was a Butterman by the long-haired mole on his fourth chin.

Bertha figured that the aliens might be able to beam individual Buttermans away but doubted that any device could handle all of them at the same time. The plan had worked, and her success had put Bertha into a rather demanding mood.

"We want all of the meatloaves, right now," she shouted. "We want you to give us some alien space stuff to prove you're real. We all want a pair of those flying sneakers. We want pictures of your planet. We want ten million dollars each. We want to rule the world."

Beula whispered something into her sister's ear.

"And we want a pony." Bertha finished the list of demands and moved directly on to one of her favorite things—the threat.

"If you don't give us everything we demand in ten seconds"—she squeezed Mr. Mueller's hand and pulled his arm up into the air—"Mr. Muleface will never cook again."

"Are you really gonna let them go if they give us what you want?" Beula whispered.

"Nah," Bertha whispered back. "But they don't know that, do they?"

"You are so smart." Beula wiggled her ears in a way that always made Bertha jealous.

Suddenly the front door of the house opened. The Buttermans stepped back at the hissing sound but kept their hands tightly clasped. Louis, Arlo, Terri, D7 and little Katherine walked out, carrying baking pans.

"That's more like it," Bertha barked. "And those meatloaves better be yummy."

"What about those other four bratniks?" Beula asked.

"Don't worry about them, they're not from outer space. We'll take care of them at school on Monday," Bertha snarled.

The captain and crew moved forward until they were less than fifteen feet from the line of Buttermans.

"Let's see your loaves," Bertha commanded.

Katherine and the rest kept walking. As they did, they slowly turned the pans until the Buttermans could see that they were . . .

"Empty?" they all screamed at once.

Katherine dropped her pan, pulled a communicator from her pocket, pushed the transmit button and ordered, "Now!"

Inside the *Meatloaf,* Ellie, BB, Joyce and Perry sat nervously at their battle stations. When the order came, they acted quickly.

"Look!" Bruno Butterman pointed while all the rest gasped, grimaced and growled. The house lifted about a foot off the ground. It started to shimmer and quiver in the air. Then, with a loud popping sound, the house hologram vanished, and the Buttermans stood face-to-thruster with the starship *Meatloaf* in all its splendor.

"Fire!" Ellie, as acting captain, ordered.

BB didn't have to be told twice. He aimed the forward phaser banks and fired.

Beams of red, yellow and blue light flashed from the *Meatloaf*. When they hit the ground in front of the Buttermans, there were explosions. Dirt flew everywhere, filling the air with dust.

Bertha and Beula let go of Mr. Mueller's arms. *"Plan B!"* Bertha shouted.

"We got a plan B?" Beula asked.

"Yes."

More phaser blasts filled the air.

"It's a good thing we do."

Bertha pulled Beula away by the mole hair. "Come on. Hurry, while they're not looking."

In the thick smoke and utter confusion of the moment, Bertha and Beula slipped away from the group and headed for the open door of the *Meatloaf*. The other Buttermans broke rank and ran in every direction. As BB continued to pour on the phaser fire, the Buttermans ran left, they ran right, they ran into each other and they ran in circles.

"Now, Joyce! Now!" Ellie shouted as soon as she saw that the crew had pulled Mr. Mueller to safety. "Beam 'em, baby!"

Joyce pushed all of the buttons and slid the slide controls on the transporter. All the Buttermans vanished from view.

Perry instantly reestablished the holographic image so that the neighbors wouldn't talk, and Ellie lowered the house back to the ground. There was a collective sigh of relief. "Where did you send them?" BB asked.

Joyce just shrugged her shoulders and said, "Away."

"Away is good," BB nodded.

"Wait a minute." Joyce was looking at her controls. "This shows that we only beamed seven Buttermans. Two are missing."

Perry did a quick video, heat, movement and odor scan of the entire area surrounding the *Meatloaf*. "Not a trace of Butterman," he reported. "Two of them must have run away before you beamed the rest."

"What's the dif?" Ellie asked. "As BB said . . . *away* is good."

"You're from when?" Louie was extremely excited about Mr. Mueller's announcement.

"The year 6859," Mr. Mueller answered. "Actually I was born in 6825, but 6859 is the time I volunteered to come here."

"For what reason?" Arlo asked.

"Your first mission failed. The Buttermans stopped you from launching by sucking the meatloaves back from the fueling tubes before you could start the starship. The time porthole closed, and you were trapped here forever."

"Yeah, I'd say that would represent failure," Louie said.

"The Buttermans made you go on talk shows and sign miniature flying saucers at carnivals. It took us seventy years to make a new *Meatloaf* and scrounge up enough uncontaminated synthochup to send me back here . . . one way."

"If you just got back here, how come you're so old and grown up?" Terri looked up at the thirty-seven-year-old teacher who was actually fifty-six years younger than she was.

"We overshot the time by twenty-five years."

"You mean you had to grow up all over again?"

"Yes." Mr. Mueller sighed. "But, it's a little easier the second time around."

"Why didn't you tell us who you were right away?" Louie asked.

"I had to be sure you were the ones I've been waiting for, for twenty-five years. I didn't want to make a mistake."

"Well, now you can come home," D7 said. "My time-displacement patches can keep you the same age while you're traveling through the centuries."

"I appreciate the offer," Mr. Mueller said, "but I can't. I have a family . . . a life. I belong here now."

"You must be kidding," Louie said, remembering the episode at the mall. "It's so barbaric."

"But it's home."

Through the entire conversation, Katherine hadn't said a word. Instead she'd just stared at Mr. Mueller as if searching for an answer in his face. Finally she broke her silence. "I have to say"—she scratched her little dimpled chin—"that from the very first time I saw you, I thought you looked somewhat familiar."

Mr. Mueller looked down at the five-year-old and smiled broadly. "I should look familiar . . . Grandma."

A short while later, after some long good-byes, the crew and passengers on the *Meatloaf* were strapped in and ready to roar. Ellie, BB, Joyce and Perry had all stuck on their time-displacement patches. Only BB wore his on his forehead. Captain Asher started the flight countdown, and the student passengers were ready for the time of their lives.

Ellie smelled something funny, but she figured maybe that was how a starship smelled before launch or that BB was having one of his "attacks." Ellie's seat was the farthest back and the closest to the storage area. It was there where two unwelcome stowaways hid. Stowaways named Beula and Bertha Butterman.

"Eight, seven, six, five," Captain Asher counted down, "four, three, two, one. Warp drive ignition, now."

"Warp drive engaged," Arlo said.

"Hang on, everyone," Captain Asher called out. "Next stop . . . the year 6789."

About the Author

Jerry Piasecki is the creative director for a Michigan advertising agency. Previously he was a radio newsperson in Detroit and New York. He has also written, directed and acted in numerous commercials, industrial films and documentaries. The writing he loves most, though, is for young readers, "where one is free to let the mind soar beyond grown-up barriers and defenses." Jerry lives in Farmington Hills, Michigan. He has a teenage daughter, Amanda, who has a dog named Rusty and a cat named Pepper.